I0735920

X-CURSE

Erase the Anomaly

BY

DIRE KEPLER

To the dreamers.

anomaly[1]

: deviation from the common rule :
IRREGULARITY

excurse[2]

: to journey or pass through,
make an excursion :

[1] "Anomaly." *Merriam-Webster.com Dictionary*, Merriam-Webster, https://www.merriam-webster.com/dictionary/anomaly.

[2] "Excurse." Merriam-Webster.com Dictionary, Merriam-Webster, https://www.merriam-webster.com/dictionary/excurse.

Table of Contents

The Cube

1

Boy 1124562 jolted awake as a delicate pressure cut through his sleep like sharpened steel. A sensor was brushing against his elbow. Recoiling from the edge of the cube wall, he breathed a soft curse into the dim glowing light of the scrolling sign posted outside his cube. He blinked away the fog of sleep and watched the numbers on the board tick forward, counting each moment of his neighbor's life. A lifetime that mirrored his own so closely that the scrolling statistics of weight and height may as well be his.

A soft, yet ominous click broke the silence and 1124562 flattened himself against his bedding. He closed his eyes and though his heart pounded inside his chest, he forced his breathing to steady as the tick and whir of a Keeper grew louder. The machine stopped at his door and shone a light into the room to inspect him. It waited for him to stir, but he wouldn't give it the satisfaction. He lay still beneath the cool beam of inspection, muscles tense beneath his tunic and waited for the Keeper to leave.

2,920 cycles ago, Boy 1124562 and his batch of brothers were animated. The last 35 of those cycles had been spent here, at the Career Aptitude Testing compound. But before this cube, with its steel walls implanted with sensors, he'd lived in the Nursery with the others. It had been a place of friendship, and innocent brotherhood, with wide open spaces to play. At night, he had slept soundly, snuggled against the warm bodies of his brothers.

But here, locked in cubes at the bottom of the testing compound they were kept separate. A pain in his chest opened so wide that it ached as he thought of the collection of individuals locked in cubes all around him, layers of locks and steel keeping them apart. He was lonely.

He hoped the ache that yawned in the space behind his ribs would disappear soon. Once this rest was over, the door would unlock, and he'd emerge to join his brothers waking to a new cycle. When he was with them, the strangeness of this place was bearable. If only sleep would come, and speed time along so he could be with his brothers again.

He tossed and turned in his cube, careful not to touch the sensors again. The first night, he had pushed against a sensor in sleepy frustration as he fought with his blanket. Almost instantly a Keeper had come to the cube door. It wasn't like when the Nannies came into the Nursery to gently lull little Boys to sleep with the rhythmic clicking and humming of their gears and circuits. The Keeper sprayed something into his cube that made his eyes heavy and caused him to gasp for air until he fell to the floor in a deep and strange sleep that made his head ache the next morning.

Instead of thrashing about and alerting a Keeper to his sleeplessness, he learned to lie quiet and still on the warm floor covered by his blanket. There was nothing to do but stare out at the pod across the hall at the pale blue scrolling statistics of Boy 1123856.

Cycles since animation... 2,920... Height... 114.3 centimeters... Weight... 25.945 kilograms ... C.A.T. Result: unknown

1124562 wasn't sure what the Career Aptitude Testing compound was for, or what the C.A.T. Result was supposed to mean. All he knew was that aside from the quiet sound of dozens of chests rising and falling in unified sleep the pod lay silent.

The stillness made him afraid.

It seemed as if he waited in silence forever before the bright tubes of white light flickered and began to glow through the thin clear panels above him. He rubbed his eyes to adjust to the bright light but continued staring at the statistics board of the Boy across the hall. It flickered and updated to read: Cycles since animation... 2,921. Boy 1124562 pushed the blanket off and sat upright in his cube, wiping the dryness out of his tired eyes.

Although his body was exhausted from another night without sleep, his senses were alert to the sights and sounds of the other Boys waking in their cubes. He heard each of them stirring from beneath identical white blankets. He imagined each of them putting away their blankets and sitting cross-legged without touching the walls as they patiently waited for breakfast.

1124562 folded his own blanket and put it away neatly behind the small square door marked *Blanket* before taking the same position in the center of his cube. He closed his eyes and listened for the familiar sounds of breakfast rolling through hollow tubes. His mouth watered as the noise of hundreds of meals tumbling over steel grew louder. The almost invisible door above him swung open and then clicked shut, depositing three perfectly round breakfast tablets into the bin on the wall marked *Food*.

"Remember, breakfast is the most important meal of the cycle. Eat up Boys, so that each of you can grow up to be big and strong." A cold-as-steel voice repeated the greeting the same way it had every morning since the Boys had arrived at C.A.T. Boy 1124562 wasn't sure where the voice came from, but he imagined it seeping out of the dozens of Keepers that patrolled the halls.

Dutifully, 1124562 picked up the tablets from the bin, put them in his mouth, and chewed them until they turned into a sticky paste against his tongue. He reached up to the ceiling of the pod and pulled down a thin retractable hose, biting the end until the cool liquid forced its way through the slit at the end of the tube. With a few silent sucks from the chute marked *Drink*, he was able to swallow his breakfast down and feel the satisfaction of a full stomach.

Once the excitement of breakfast had passed, there was nothing to do but wait for one of the Keepers to let him out of the cube so that he could get ready for class. 1124562 sat perfectly still, closing his eyes and regulating his breathing to stay as quiet as possible. He craved the moment when the Keeper would tell him what a good Boy he had been and let him out into the Dressing Hall. Not only did being a good Boy make him happy, but he'd also get to finally relieve himself and change into a fresh set of clothes.

Not long after he first arrived, 1124562 discovered that Boys who fussed or complained weren't let out of their cubes. Instead, they were sprayed down with the sticky fog that forced them to sleep. The second time he got fogged, it was because he begged the Keeper to let him out before the scheduled time. During the night, he drank too much liquid and had to relieve himself so much that it hurt. The Keeper didn't respond to his cries with help and concern; it merely sprayed him. Almost immediately, he'd fallen into a crumple on the floor only to wake up later covered in his own soil and stink.

"Bad Boys aren't allowed in class," one of the Keepers had told him the next cycle when the sensors in his cube alerted it that he was awake. Unlike a few of the other Boys in his pod who were sprayed many times before learning their lesson, 1124562 vowed that he would never act out again.

The time finally came for the Keepers to roll across the hard floors on their shiny polished wheels and open the doors to the cubes. One of them stopped in front of 1124562's door and put its arm into the data lock just outside. The Keeper's eyes blinked yellow and blue as it downloaded the data from the previous night and then shone bright green.

"You've been a very good Boy, 1124562. Welcome to cycle number 2,921. Please make your way to the Dressing Hall and prepare for class."

The Keeper unlocked the door and 1124562 waited until it moved away from his cube before he felt comfortable leaving the tight space. Once he heard it speaking to the Boy in the next cube over, he crawled through the low door and stood up straight in the hallway. He stretched his arms and legs as far as they would go and nodded a silent hello to the other Boys spilling into the hall.

A shrill scream cut through the quiet bustle of the morning as a Keeper sprayed mist into one of the cubes. 1124562 and the other Boys pretended not to hear and silently began walking away from the cries of the Boy who had not behaved. It was only a moment before the fog took effect and the hall fell silent again, aside from the muted voices of Keepers unlocking doors and the quiet shuffle of bare feet against cement.

The Boys spilled into the hall, flowing quickly towards the dressing area. As 1124562 followed the mass of brothers ahead of him, he looked up. High above them was the long tube system that had brought them breakfast. The delivery system was beautiful; dozens of tubes running the length of the hall at just enough of an incline to keep the food rolling towards the cubes. A scanner at each intersection counted portions for each meal before allowing the tablets to fall into the feeder of the Boy below. It then signaled the tiny trap door to shut so that the tablets behind it could continue their course to Boys farther down the line. The tube system ended abruptly at the door to the Dressing Hall.

Still deep in thought about the feed system, he entered one of many lines for fresh clothes. The line moved quickly as each Boy passed through the scanning system that identified their number, checked their body for injuries or illness, and then dropped fresh clothes into a bin at the front of the line.

Obediently, 1124562 took the clean clothes assigned to him and moved farther into the cavernous room. He filed into another line for the shower. When it was his turn, he slipped out of his tunic and stood rigid while he was washed vigorously from head to toe by a Shower Assistant. The moment the icy cold water stopped, a blast of hot air engulfed him to dry him off. Once he was scanned again to ensure he was clean, he stepped into lightweight pants and smock and moved toward the exit so another Boy could do the same.

1124562 wondered what happened to the dirty clothes when he dropped them into a bottomless basket near the Dressing Hall's exit. He didn't have time to ponder the fate of the soiled clothes for long though; the moment he passed through the narrow opening he was crowded by his brothers as they pushed down the long and dimly lit tunnel that led to the school.

The tunnel was narrow with a ceiling so low that Boy 1124562 had to fight the urge to reach up and touch it. He knew if he did, the sensors would react, and Transportation Aides would emerge from their places hidden behind panels that blended into the walls. They would snatch him out of the group and whisk him away to an unseen corridor where he could be reprimanded. The problem with fogging a Boy in the tunnel was that the grey mist was hard to direct and could easily be breathed by good Boys standing nearby. The threat of the Machines kept 1124562 from acting out many of his urges and prevented him from exploring the hidden corridors and shiny contraptions that piqued his curiosity.

His skin crawled at the thought of the Machines touching him with their spongy rubber hands, fingers covered in silent sensors, pulling data as they tracked over his skin. A shiver ran through him as he remembered the chill of their breath, fanning out from their faces with a metallic smell. Some of them appeared almost indistinguishable from Men until they came close enough, then he could smell hydraulics lurking beneath their synthetic skin and see the ticking gears moving behind the glass in their perfectly formed eyes.

Boy 1124562 knew that the Machines were his superiors, so he fought the urge to squirm or run away when they came near him. Anything that might be interpreted as disobedience was rewarded with the sticky sleep-spray. While most of the Boys found themselves returned to their cube when they woke, some Boys hadn't been seen again in the pod.

Ever.

1124562 felt a wave of relief when he finally reached the door to his classroom and was able to break away from the crowd. He took a couple of deep breaths before ambling over to his desk and taking a seat.

Until C.A.T., 1124562 had only seen a Man once before, so he had been surprised on the first day of class to enter the room and see one again. Each of the curious students had fought back the urge to bombard the old human with questions, sitting politely at their desks with curiosity burning inside of them like roaring fires. The Man's low number, 2871, was proof that he was very old. He must have been animated tens of thousands of cycles before the group he now taught. 1124562 was sure he hadn't been the only one staring at the Man's long black robe and wiry hair sprouting out unnaturally from his face instead of growing atop his head.

This cycle, each of the Boys took their seats in front of their assigned tablets. One by one their faces relaxed, and they began to talk openly to each other. 1124562 kept to himself though, consumed with watching 2871 as he scrolled through the cycle's tests.

The Man found what he was looking for and flicked his wrist to push it from the tablet in his lap and onto the wall behind him. The wall was not like the cold metallic walls in the other rooms. It glowed steadily white and functioned just like the tablets. 2871 touched the wall without fear or hesitation, and the wall responded by altering the projected image according to the direction of his hands. 1124562 ached to become as confident and unafraid as the Man before him.

Once the last Boy was seated, 2871 turned to face the class. "This cycle, dear Boys, before we begin our tests, I thought we would have a brief discussion. I am sure that by now you have become accustomed to the routine in your pods and learned to behave like good Boys." 2871 sat down in the high-backed chair hovering at the front of the room and folded his arms against his chest. "But I am also sure that you have had time to form questions, thoughts, and concerns about what you are doing here, about Adaline, and the Community at large."

Most of the Boys fidgeted, staring at their blank tablets and stealing quick uncertain glances around the room but 1124562 immediately touched the button on his tablet indicating that he had a question.

"Before I answer any questions, let me say that I have no intention of calling you each by your very long identification numbers." The teacher looked briefly at the list of student numbers and groaned. "They seem to get longer with every class, and my mind just can't keep up. Instead, I will call you by your last two digits, and I ask that you please do the same. You, 62," the Man touched his own tablet to quiet 1124562's blinking light on the projected screen behind him. "What is your question?"

"What is Career Aptitude Testing?"

"Ah, a wonderful question to begin our discussion." The Man looked intently into the face of each student before speaking again, creating a lengthy pause, making the Boys stare back at him in nervous anticipation. "Each of you has his own unique talents. Although we all look the same at animation, we each carry our own strengths and weaknesses. This compound is a place where Boys learn to live separately and are tested to find what those individual strengths and weaknesses are. When you complete your testing and basic function training, you will be sorted into careers and will be trained to work for the betterment of Adaline."

Instantly the projected tablet began to flash with questions from the other Boys. "18, what is your question?"

A Boy on the other end of the room asked quickly, "What is Adaline?"

The teacher's face broke into a soft, warm smile. The curves of his face were very unlike the rigid grins of the Keepers. His eyes closed as his cheeks lifted and his eyebrows rose, causing the Boys to smile automatically in return. "Adaline is everything, dear Boy. It is the ground beneath your feet and the nitrogen-oxygen blend in your lungs. It is the world we exist in. It spans many kilometers in every direction, home to thousands of pods and compounds just like this one. But Adaline is more than just this place where we live. It is also the intricate network tying every sensor and Machine together, watching over us and anticipating our every need."

"Is Adaline alive?" 18 asked.

71 stroked the wild white hair erupting from his chin, a thoughtful expression dancing across his face. "Adaline isn't a living thing, like you or I, but it is intelligent. It collects the data from everything we do and uses that information to decide where we belong and how we can best serve the Community."

The next Boy piped in, without waiting for his number to be called. "What is the Community?"

"The Community is our governing body. It lays out the rules and structure that we follow. If you think of the Community as a giant Machine, we humans are the gears and pistons that make the Machine work. Each of us has a different function, but we all work together to keep the Machine moving smoothly. The real Machines that guide us: Keepers, Assistants, Aides, and others that you will meet are like the circuits that command each of the gears and pistons to move and sense when there is a malfunction in the system." 71's voice broke as he glanced at the wall behind him. "99, what is your question?"

"What is a career, and how do we know what to do with it?"

"A career is a job function. It is your individual contribution within the Community. My job function, for example, is that of Teacher. When I was a Boy…" A quick gasp filled the room, interrupting 71's explanation. He burst out in laughter and looked around the room to the wide-eyed astonishment of the Boys around him. "Well, I may be old, but I was a Boy once! Yes, just like you, I was young and full of my own questions. When it was my time to be tested, I was given the career of Teacher, and I have performed my function for more cycles than I care to count."

The screen on the wall flashed again with questions from throughout the room. "Boy 57, let's give your question a go."

"What happened to you to make you look like… like *THAT*?"

"Oh surely, I don't look that bad. My Assistant even prompted me to comb my beard when I woke. I'm assuming that you mean how did I get to be so tall, dashingly handsome, and well dressed?"

Boy 57 shrugged his shoulders and looked around the room for guidance from his peers. All the other Boys looked equally confused.

"Well," 71 replied without waiting for an answer from the group, "It's simple. I grew up, just as each of you is bound to do sooner or later. Oh, don't you worry," he winked one eye at 57, "It doesn't happen overnight. It takes a very long time for you to reach your full potential as a Man. We humans have been given a talent that none of the Machines around us have learned to mimic—we change in time. Yes, we will stay in our assigned careers and follow the Community directive throughout our life span. But we will do so as we grow taller, bigger, stronger, weaker, smaller, smarter, sillier, and any other number of things that we can be."

The blinking on the wall behind the old human never ceased, even increasing as he moved on to new questions. "94, what would you like to add to the discussion?"

"How many careers are there? Which ones are the best ones? How do we get a good one?"

"Oh, my," the Man rubbed the facial hair he had referred to as a 'beard' and scratched where a chin would be. "Three questions from you. Well, let's see if we can answer them before we run out of time. First, there are hundreds of careers available to humans, but generally they fall into three categories. Education, Defense, and Labor. As far as which one is the best, that is something that Men continue to debate even until they are living their final cycle. In truth, all of them are essential to the Community, and so each of them can easily be argued as being the best. As far as getting a career, it will be assigned to you by the Head Machine at the end of your time at C.A.T. based on the talents and strengths that are uncovered during testing."

Although easily apparent that the Boys were still bursting with questions, the tone signaling that testing had not started on time rang through the air. "This discussion has, I trust, been enlightening. Let us resume our testing. If you have any questions that have not been answered, please hold them until our next opportunity to speak as a class. It helps to keep me from having to repeat myself twenty times." The Man made a series of motions on his tablet and in unison the wall behind him and the tablets in the hands of each Boy began to shift and change.

The tests intrigued 62. There had not been any instruction on what to do with them during any of the classes since he arrived at C.A.T. and for the first two cycles all he did was stare at the shifting images on the wall. In time, he noticed patterns in the designs and began to select and manipulate them on the tablet in front of him. He found that pushing some of them together created a variety of reactions. Whether a change in color, a sporadic explosion of lines and curves, or simply an enlarging of the image, he quickly discovered he could get an effect with nearly every stroke of his hand upon the screen.

As abruptly as the shifting shapes had appeared on the tablets, when class ended, the images on the wall and all the individual tablets in the room went dark. By the time the Boys realized that their tablets had turned off, the tones signaling the end of class were echoing through the halls and the Man had already tucked his own tablet into his robe and exited the room.

Boy 62 pushed his tablet into the drawer marked *Student Tablet* and rushed into the tunnel to follow his teacher. 2871 strode forcefully against a sea of Boys pouring out of classrooms, and 62 did his best to push after him through the crowd. He hoped to see where the Man went at the end of class—in fact, he was filled with an overwhelming urge to discover if there were more Men in the compound, and to know if they lived freely or if they were bound to the same cramped cubes as the Boys.

Although 2871 was several heads taller than the crowd pushing past him, he quickly vanished into the sea of faces. Unable to make any headway against the strength of his brothers, 62 had no choice but to reverse course and follow the flow of bodies back to their pods. He sighed in resignation.

There was nothing to do but swallow down dinner and wait for tomorrow.

The Fog

2

Time passed in a blur of Machines, testing, and dark hours spent confined. It took many cycles for 62 to adjust to his new surroundings but he finally learned to quiet his mind enough to sleep when the lights dimmed. Then, as the thickness of dinner filled his belly, slumber came quickly. He could now sleep until the sounds of breakfast rolling through the steel tubes above welcomed a new cycle.

As much as he missed the Nursery, 62 looked forward to going to class. In the cycles following the classroom discussion with 71, there had been no further talk about the role of humans in the Community or instruction on how Boys could become Men. Hopefully, his teacher would open the floor to questions again soon.

In the meantime, the tests changed from shifting shapes and lines to long lists of simple problems. At least, 62 thought they were simple. Regardless of the type of problem: terminology questions, equations, or detailed schematics, the answers seemed to leap out at him. It was almost as if the solutions were being handed to him. Neither the tablet nor the teacher ever told the Boys if they had completed the tests correctly, but 62 rarely worried about whether or not he was making mistakes. While he selected answer after answer without pause, most of the other Boys in the class seemed to scratch their heads and look around the room anxiously between questions.

The time spent sitting at his tablet surrounded by the silence of other Boys deep in thought allowed 62's mind to wander from the task at hand. His head frequently flooded with questions that he ached to ask his teacher. He didn't have a way to record his inquiries as they arrived though, so he repeated them over and over to himself until he was sure he had them memorized.

In spite of this curiosity, or perhaps because of it, Boy 62 fell into a pattern of rushing through his tests. Finishing long before the other Boys, he spent the rest of the time in class tracing his finger across the tablet while he thought about the questions mulling around in his mind. A soft grey line followed his finger as he dragged it across the smooth surface, staying for only a few moments before fading back into the tablet's white background. It didn't take long for 62 to begin moving his finger wildly across the tablet. He found that by moving quickly enough, he could create whole shapes. He began filling the tablet with pictures so quickly that there would be no more room on the screen, and he would have to wait for the lines to fade before he could make any more.

Some of the shapes he created made him feel excited and happy. But he fought the urge to show them to the Boys sitting near him for fear that he would be disciplined. Misbehaving outweighed the desire to share his creations. So, he smiled to himself instead and did his best to memorize each image before it disappeared.

When the tone sounded for class to end, 62 sighed in disappointment. He loved everything about class, the mystery of his teacher, the varying complexity of his tests, and the chance to play with the subtle images on his tablet.

He began to hope that his tests would place him in Education so that he could become a teacher like 71.

A full seven cycles after the teacher had initially opened the floor for questions, 71 again sat in his high-backed chair facing the Boys. His long beard wagged back and forth as he turned his head, his gaze following each Boy's path as he entered the room and sat behind his tablet. Once the door slid closed and the distinct clicking of the locks was heard, the teacher's eyes twinkled wildly. He cleared his throat and asked, "Well, what have we learned?"

Lights flashed on the wall behind the old human, but he didn't turn to look at the numbers displayed behind him or glance down to see who had indicated their answer on the tablet on the desk in front of him. Instead, 2871 got up slowly from his seat and began walking up and down the rows between the Boys. "I trust that you've learned a few things about the testing. First, that there are no correct answers, or even if there are correct answers, you won't be disciplined for answering incorrectly."

2871 stopped by a Boy two rows over from 62 and gazed at him knowingly. "In fact, it seems that at least one of you has purposefully answered every problem incorrectly just to find out what will happen."

The Boy beside the teacher flushed a deep red, embarrassment easily read on his face before he ducked his head and looked at his feet.

71 laughed loudly, louder than any of the Boys had heard laughter before. He slapped the Boy beside him heartily on the back and cheered, "It is always a joy when I find the ones who push the limits!" 2871 turned to the rest of the room with a stern and warning glare, "But be warned, my brothers, you will find that persistently failing your tests will not end well for you. These tests lay out the course of your future in its entirety. None of you wants to be stuck cleaning old manuals and dusting off gears for the rest of your lives. You are all much too bright for that!"

He patted the head of the blushing Boy as he continued to pace the room, and the Boy exhaled a deep sigh of relief as the teacher moved on. The Man fell silent as he allowed his warning to sink into the young minds.

"So what else have we learned?" 2871 asked the question more to himself than to the students as he continued his lecture. "Perhaps we have learned that we are able to solve problems we have never had to solve before? Some of you have shown considerable proficiency in diagnosing programming issues, which is a skill that comes in handy no matter what career you are chosen for." The teacher nodded towards 62 and the Boy sitting in front of him as he spoke these words. "And the rest of you," he opened his arms wide as if he were going to embrace the entire room, "You each will show your talents in the many cycles to come."

The Man smiled at the room, his thick eyebrows and long beard rearranging themselves with the changes in his expression. "So, that brings us to what I know you're all holding back. Are there any questions?"

Lights flashed, covering the tablet projection with blinking indicators for every Boy. "Well, I suppose that should keep us busy for the rest of the cycle," the Man said emphatically as he gestured to the wall. "Let's get started, shall we? In order of appearance on the screen, ask your question. Starting with 94. Go ahead, Brother."

The Boy looked at his teacher with a look of deep concentration, "Last time, you said we are animated all the same, but we have different talents. How can we be the same as well as different?"

"Excellent question, 94. What better place to start to learn about ourselves than at the beginning! How many of you know what the animation process is?" The teacher paused for just a moment until he was sure none of the Boys had an answer. "Of course, I didn't expect any of you to know the process. Your Nannies would have no reason to educate you. So, let us begin.

"In order to animate a human, two forms of matter are joined. This combining of matter results in the simultaneous division of cells that are so small that they cannot be seen outside of the Laboratory. The Laboratory, of course, is where animation is conducted.

"Over time, the cells divide and grow so much that they begin to form a body, and that body grows until it is about the size of your fist." At this he folded the long slender fingers of his right hand until his hand resembled a tight ball of flesh and raised it in the air for the whole class to see. "At this point, the being is not able to breathe or feed on its own. In fact, it's completely dependent on the Animators to keep it alive.

"All of the organs and essential tissues continue to form inside this body and the being grows at an incredible rate until it is roughly the size of your head." Instinctively, all the Boys began to look around the room, judging the sizes of their brother's identical heads and trying to imagine a body so small.

"Eventually, the body is fully formed and able to function independent of the Animator's assistance, so they cease feeding it, expel it from its protective casing and ship it to the Nursery where it grows and becomes…" the teacher waved his hands wildly around the room, "one of you. Now, because of this process, the indistinguishable tissue used and identical procedures for each Boy's creation, physically we all appear very much the same. We each have the same brown hair, same pink skin, same brown eyes and same bone and muscle structure. But that is where the similarities end. Each of us has our own mind, our own likes and dislikes, our own strengths and weaknesses, our own wants and desires. So therefore, we are all the same. But we are each different as well."

The next Boy on the screen, 75, quietly asked his question as the others excitedly poked and pulled at their skin and hair, realizing for the first time that each of them looked identical to the Boys sitting around them. Even 62 was so caught up in the excitement of comparing his bare toes to those of his neighbor that he missed it.

"Fantastic question, 75!" The teacher's exclamation prompted the Boys to break away from their inspection of one another. "The reason that you must sleep alone in your own cube is that you are growing to become Men. Studies have shown, time and again, that Men are the most productive if they are kept alone during rest and come together as a group to solve problems. I know it is lonely, little one, but you will eventually get used to it."

62 now had his turn to ask the teacher a question, and he sorted through the dozens of possibilities in his mind. He quickly identified the one that bothered him the most. "What happens to the Boys in our pod who misbehave and then never come back from their discipline?"

The room fell silent, each of the Boys freezing in the many odd poses they'd configured during their comparison of one another. Regardless of their odd position, each Boy turned eyes full of burning desire and sorrow towards the teacher.

Someone near the door chimed in, "Yes, what happens to them?"

A Boy in the back of the room added, "Are they all right?"

A tentative voice near the teacher whispered, "Will they ever come back?"

The teacher's expression changed from enthusiasm to sadness, and he turned his back quickly on the Boys. "This is not a question that I have the answer to. Boys and Men will disappear from your lives when they are found to be acting against the best interest of the Community. No one knows why they decide to no longer work beside their brothers, but when they make that choice, they are taken from us, and we must learn to continue on without them."

A somber grief filled the room as the group mourned the loss of brothers who would never again return to their pod. The teacher remained standing with his back to the class for many long minutes. Finally, he cleared his throat loudly and addressed the class again, a slight crack in his voice. "Enough of such talk. Let us think on more cheerful things. 18, what is your question?"

The questions and answers continued on until the end of the class but 62 didn't hear the other Boys or his teacher any longer. The sound that rang between his ears was the sobbing cries of the Boys he would never see again. His chest ached as he thought of them being sprayed with the sticky fog of sleep and taken away forever.

Although he didn't know much about the differences between humans and Machines, he was sure that it must be difficult or impossible to reprogram a malfunctioning human. 62 had seen dozens of Machines repaired in the Nursery and at C.A.T. Machines were worked on out in the open when they broke down, it being easier for repairs to be done at the site of the problem than to lug broken equipment somewhere else to fix. But 62 had never seen repairs done on a human before. He realized that the organs and tissues 71 described during the explanation of animation must take specialized equipment to handle. He had heard of broken Machines being disassembled and discarded…he hoped that this was not the way that the misbehaving Boys and Men were handled.

The thought of his brothers being ripped apart or reprogrammed troubled 62 deeply, and for the rest of the cycle he was lost in thought over the concept. He was relieved when the quiet tones signaled it was time to return to the pods. It would take a long time alone for him to clear his head.

Sleep did not come for 62 that night, and he wondered how his brothers in the adjacent cubicles were able to close their eyes and drift off to sleep without worry. Fear coursed through his veins, and each time his eyes did grow heavy enough for sleep to overtake him he was jolted awake by the images of angry Keepers flickering behind his eyelids.

As he had when he first arrived at C.A.T., 62 rolled onto his side and looked up at the scrolling sign above the doorway of the cube across the walkway.

Cycles since animation... 2,937... Height...
117.3   centimeters... Weight... 26.012
kilograms ... C.A.T. Result: unknown.

X-CURSE

The Heat

3

It took many cycles for 62's concern for the missing Boys to fade, but eventually the mind-numbing schedule of continuous testing drowned out the feeling of sadness. The fear that he might do something bad and be pulled out of his pod was present enough, however, to cause him to behave as perfectly as he could. The threat of being taken away also stirred a new curiosity. He began to wonder about what might exist beyond C.A.T.

No longer so grief-stricken that he stared at his feet, he began to steal lengthy glances at his teacher. He thought about the old Man moving down the halls of a pod as a Boy thousands of cycles ago. It was strange to think that the hair on 62's own head would migrate down to cover his chin and cheeks the way that they masked his teacher's face. But, as 2871 pointed out during the last classroom discussion, each Boy and Man were created equally and from the same synthesized matter. None would ever rise above the station of any of the others, and all would grow to be grey Men; tall and lean under their bristly white facial hair. He spread out his thick, chubby hand and couldn't imagine it turning into slender fingers and folds of loose skin.

He was still too young to grasp the complications and simplicities brought on by the sameness he shared with his brothers, but he was beginning to sense a familiar connection with them and a new desire to understand *why* they were each created the same. He found himself not only in awe of his masterful teacher, but also compelled to find other teachers that tutored the thousands of Boys in C.A.T.

Finding other Men turned out to be difficult; getting close enough to speak to them was impossible. Whenever he caught a glimpse of a distant Man wandering at the far end of the tunnel, he would vanish in the time it took for 62 to pick his way through the crowd, just as when he had tried to follow his own teacher after class.

One cycle, 62 even tried pretending to be lost, wandering into a classroom that was not his own. Before he so much as set foot in the room, a strange tingling feeling flowed down his back causing a foreign fluttering in his chest so unsettling it stopped him dead in his tracks. He had to push himself against a wall in the hallway to steady himself before doubling over to catch his breath. The feeling stopped as quickly as it had come, so he thought he must have imagined it, and attempted to enter the room again. The tingling overwhelmed him again, stronger this time. The sudden pulse in his internal organs startled him enough that he did not make a third attempt.

The more hurdles he discovered to finding answers to his many questions, the more 62's mind sprang forward into new areas of curiosity. The question that plagued him the most frequently was, "Why?"

Why was he unable to find a Man to answer all of his questions at once? Why was he spending so much time tapping away at a tablet filled with problems? Why was he unable to enter another classroom? Why was he so unhappy following his directive to test into a career function?

And more importantly, why did all the other Boys seem to be so content?

Waves of heat spread beneath his skin, building and growing more intense as the cycles passed. Between the silent testing and segregated hours in the pods, 62 was feeling restless. The heat sensation was unfamiliar to him, and it caused his entire body to feel as rigid as the steel walls that enveloped him. There was an unsettling tenseness in his bones, and he wondered if he were transforming into a Machine from the inside-out.

Maybe this was how Machines were made.

The changes in 62 did not go unnoticed. The Keepers passed by the door of his cube more frequently during his rest periods, downloading his data anew with each pass.

"There, there," the mechanical voices cooed through the thin wires of the door, "That's a good Boy." Although the Keepers each smiled their rigid smiles and said only kind words to him, 62 couldn't help but feel that they were waiting for him to misbehave so that they could spray him with fog and take him away.

The truth was 62 felt like misbehaving. The more the fear of what might be lurking beyond the walls of C.A.T. grew, the more frequently he had to fight the urge to be bad. He could picture himself throwing his fists through the thin synthetic skin of the Keepers and raking at their internal mechanisms with fury. He sometimes found himself staring at the seams in the walls or the thin vents lining the ceiling of the pod, wondering if he might be strong enough to rip through them to get to the darkness on the other side. As the desire to hit other Boys, smash his tablet, and rip his blanket became stronger, he became more afraid. 62 began crossing his arms when he walked and crossing his legs when he sat in an attempt to keep them from doing the bad things in his mind.

62 had felt calm and comfortable before he had been transported to C.A.T. and Boys began disappearing from their pods. Now, the constant threat of losing another misbehaving brother, and the fear that he might misbehave

himself, caused him to have difficulty controlling his feelings and actions.

He did his best to hide the bad thoughts, and he believed that he was doing a fair job of it until the end of a particularly difficult cycle of testing. As he was pretending to be preoccupied with an error produced by thousands of lines of code, 62 suddenly felt the weight of his teacher's gaze upon him. Quickly, he moved his hands to the margins of the equations, covering the pictures he had created on his tablet and hoped that they would dissolve before 71 could see them. 62 looked up to find the teacher making slow strides toward his desk.

62 stifled a sigh of relief as the images on the tablet faded into the white background just before his teacher loomed above him.

71 leaned down until his mouth was level with 62's left ear and spoke in a soft whisper. "I would be much obliged if you would conference with me outside."

A blank stare was the only response that 62 was able to muster. He had never seen any of the other Boys leave the classroom before the end of testing. He fidgeted slightly in his seat and pushed his tablet toward the edge of the desk. He sat on his hands and looked up at the teacher while deciding whether or not to comply with the request.

"Really, it will only take a few moments, and I trust that you will find the conversation most enlightening." 71 didn't wait for a response and simply walked towards the exit. He passed his hand along the seam of the door and the lock clicked. The sliding steel door hissed on hydraulics. After he passed through, the door remained open.

The other Boys looked on as 62 got up and walked past them, curiously staring to see what would happen to him. 62 smiled in what he hoped was a calm expression and moved toward the door. His nervousness prompted his feet to trip over one another, and there was a loud crash as his knee caught the edge of a hover chair. The chair faltered under his weight and careened into the side of a neighboring desk.

The teacher's head and shoulders became visible around the corner of the still open doorway, his beard wagging as he stifled a small laugh. He called out, "Hurry now, we don't have all the time in Adaline to waste."

"Yes, Teacher," 62 muttered under his breath as he pulled the hover chair and desk out of their entanglement and slid them back to their proper positions. He apologized to the Boys that his fall had disrupted. As carefully and quietly as possible, he made his way through the remainder of the classroom under the watchful gaze of his brothers. He was relieved when the door finally slid closed behind him with a loud hiss.

The relief was short lived. As the embarrassment of his uncoordinated exit melted from his consciousness, the looming dark mass of the teacher replaced it. 71 stood just inches from 62, his bulky robes and long grey hair seeming to push all of the nitrogen and oxygen from the atmosphere around him. 62 pressed himself against the cold steel of the wall behind him, more worried about the Man in front of him than the sensors that would begin scanning the second his skin made contact.

"Don't look so frightened. I'm really quite harmless." 71 crossed his arms and adjusted himself until his beard lay over his forearms like a living blanket.

"What… why are we out here?" 62 could feel tingling in the tips of his fingers where the scanners had found him. He worried that he and the teacher might not be allowed outside of the classroom and quickly pulled away from the wall.

"I wanted to speak with you about some changes in your behavior that I've noticed." The old Man spoke softly, watching as Boy 62 shuffled uneasily. "It appears that there is something bothering you, and it has been affecting some of your testing results."

62 hadn't considered that his moments of trailing thoughts might be affecting his tests. He was still finishing them far earlier than any of the other Boys, and even with the distraction of his thoughts didn't feel that they had

become any more challenging. In fact, they seemed to be getting easier.

"I don't understand what happened with the testing, but I'm sorry if I have been performing below standard." 62 felt the smooth fabric of his smock between his fingertips and willed the cloth fibers to erase the strange sensation that remained after touching the scanners. "What can I do to be a better Boy?"

71 looked intently down on his student. He sighed and uncrossed his arms. Placing one hand on his hip, and the other softly on the small Boy's shoulder he said quietly, "Honestly there is little that you can do. You are testing well, and I will be surprised if you don't test into one of the higher levels of Education or Defense when all is said and done. What I am really worried about are the pictures that you make when your tests are complete."

Boy 62 felt his stomach churn. His eyes grew wide, and his mouth dropped open, but no words escaped. He hadn't known that anyone would be able to see the images. "I – I didn't mean to… I just always finish the testing with so much time left." 62 stumbled over his words as he tried to explain his actions, even though he didn't fully understand them himself.

The teacher looked over one shoulder and then the other, ensuring that there was no one but the ever-present wall sensors to record him. Once satisfied, he kneeled down until his eyes were level with the Boy quivering before him. "It's alright," he whispered quietly. "No one has seen the pictures but me. I erase them before sending the tests out to the Head Machine for review. The Machines have never had any interest in the creativity of humans at any age, and I doubt even if they saw them that they would add them into your data file. I only have wondered why they have changed."

"Changed?" Boy 62 looked onto the Man through the blurriness of tear-filled eyes. "I'm not in trouble? Oh…" he looked down at the floor somberly and then back at his teacher. "You mean, the *disassembly*?"

"Yes," 71 nodded. "Violent disassembly. Before, you seemed to be drawing random shapes and Boys. As if you were recreating friendly dreams."

"Dreams?"

"Oh, dear. Forgive me. I forget just how little your generation is being taught now. The definition of 'dream' is 'A series of images, ideas, emotions, and sensations occurring involuntarily in the mind during certain stages of sleep.' Dreams are pictures people used to see after they closed their eyes in a sleeping rest. They are a rarity now. Very few of us experience them." He considered 62 with a curious expression. "Does any of this make sense to you?"

62 nodded. "I see things when I rest. I know it's not… normal. Do you dream, too?"

"I do. Now, as I was saying, your drawings seemed to be pictures of happy dreams. Of Boys you might have known and places you might be imagining." The man shifted slightly as the strain of kneeling pricked at his old knees.

"Drawing?" None of what the teacher was saying made sense.

"Mother Dustblower!" The teacher yelled, pounding his free hand firmly against the floor and shaking his head in frustration. "Drawing. The action of moving your hand or stylus across the screen and creating images with one or more lines. We really aren't teaching you anything, are we?"

Boy 62's face became frozen save the quick flutter of his eyelashes as he blinked in astonishment. He repeated quietly, "I draw, and I dream. I draw, and I dream. I draw… and I *dream*…"

"Yes, yes," the teacher's face had started to become puffy and red with the strain of staying at eye level with his student and the frustration of realizing that the child knew so little of his own capabilities. "But why such change over time? Why the disassembly?"

"I have heat," Boy 62 replied frankly. He pointed to the center of his chest with his index finger. "I feel it here. It boils and burns, and it makes me want to… *to disassemble.*” He whispered the last of the sentence, understanding the gravity of what might happen if the Keepers knew that he longed to scrape the tiny gears from their eyes and pull at their hydraulic hoses until they burst.

The old Man nodded silently for a moment, then with great effort pushed himself up off the floor until he was again standing at his full height. “I think I understand. This heat, it came after we discussed the Keepers disciplining your brothers and taking them away?”

“Yes, and when I think about the fog.” Boy 62 wondered if 71 felt the heat too. “I feel the heat and it fills me up like the fog, except after it fills me up, I don’t want to sleep. I want to disassemble them.”

Another Man walked across the far end of the hallway, checking on the entrance to another set of pods. 71 turned to face him, waving his hand in the air in a form of greeting. The other Man did the same in return and disappeared through a distant classroom door. Without turning around to face 62 the teacher said quickly, “Class is about to end, and you will need to go back to your pod. However, I am going to put in a request to the Head Machine to allow me to tutor you for one hour following class from now on. It is very important that if anyone asks you about these tutoring lessons that you tell them you are learning about coolant systems and Defense Mechanics. Do you understand?”

Boy 62 stared at the back of his teacher’s robes, and if anyone had looked at his confused expression, they would have known that he didn’t understand at all. But for some reason he felt that it was very important to answer with, “Yes, I understand.”

The tones played quietly in the classrooms, the sound pushing its way through the tight seams of dozens of closed doors. Before 62 could muster the courage to ask what a tutoring lesson was, the doors all slid open with a quick hiss and Boys flooded the tunnel as they marched back to their pod.

The Mistake

4

62 lay in the darkness of his cube and went over his brief conversation with 71. The things he was experiencing had *names*. That meant that other Boys and Men must have experienced them before. Drawing and dreaming had come to him without any effort. Although he was nervous that his teacher might inform the Machines about this, and the Machines might decide that he was being bad, he was glad there was someone he could share them with.

As he stared at the ceiling above him, the glow of the scrolling data of the Boy across the hall reflected on the thin light panel embedded above him. His fingers traveled against the warm floor, absently drawing invisible swirls and lines. When he realized his fingers were drawing, he closed his eyes and pretended to see the lines extending beyond his fingertips, transforming into ragged shapes and then melding into a series of gears and circuits.

He froze when a Keeper patrolled the hall outside his door. The thought of its mechanical components, gears and circuits, all designed to watch him brought the heat back to his chest. The boiling sensation flowed under his skin until it was so hot that he felt he might burn up. One of the Nannies in the Nursery had once caught fire when a Boy accidentally urinated on its charging pack during their toilet training phase. The Machine had sputtered a bit and then sparks could be seen in its joints before it suddenly caught fire. Several of the other Nannies surrounded it, simultaneously pushing the Boys back from the blaze and dousing the burning Machine in an inflammable powder. Once the fire was out, a Man, who looked thousands of cycles younger than 71, had come to repair the broken Nanny. He explained to the Boys what had happened as he quickly repaired it. If he burst into flame, 62 wondered if they would send a Man to repair *him*.

62 raised his hands to his face and examined them in the faint blue light from the hall. They were softer than the hands of the Keepers. He didn't have any exposed joints or circuits; instead, his skin stretched across his organic frame in one continuous sheath. The more he learned about himself, the more new questions bounced against one another inside his mind.

He turned his thoughts away from the Machines and again concentrated on what his teacher had said about drawing, dreaming, and tutoring. He closed his eyes tight and thought about the dreams he had experienced the last few nights. He couldn't remember more than a few flashes of them, but as he concentrated on the friendly faces and the comfort of the Nursery that filled them, he could feel the heat in his chest start to cool.

He wondered sleepily about the tutoring. Because he'd never heard the word before, he had no concept of what it might be, but his mind wandered into visions of 71 and himself drawing on tablets and showing them to one another on the large projection wall. A small smile crept across his lips as he drifted off into a deep sleep.

When the sounds of breakfast rolling through feeder tubes rang in his ears and the flickering lights above him began to shine through his eyelids, 62 sprang up with excitement and energy. The heat that had filled him the night before had been replaced with cool assurance. Long before the Keepers began opening doors to the pods, he had stuffed his poorly folded blanket into its bin and had almost choked on his breakfast by swallowing it too quickly. He was able to sit in his appointed spot in the center of the cube, but not without wiggling his toes and tapping his fingers against his knees in excited anticipation.

He nearly toppled over the Keeper that unlocked the door and had to hold himself back to keep from running into his brothers as he anxiously wove through the sleepy mass headed toward the Dressing Hall. He got irritated with the Shower Assistant for taking too long and was in such a hurry that he grabbed the wrong tunic before he ran toward the exit. He bounded through the crowd completely unaware that he was wearing dirty clothes. Luckily, Boy 99 caught him by the arm before he stepped through the door and out into the tunnel.

"62! You're not dressed! Don't you know you can't wear a dirty tunic to class?" 99 spun 62 around so that he was facing the rows of Boys and Shower Assistants that he had just fled. "You're going to get yourself sprayed running around like that."

"Oh, yeah. Thanks." 62 shook his head and tried to focus. "Do you think my clean smock and pants are still around somewhere?"

"I don't know," 99 said quickly, "I've never seen anyone leave them behind before. Let's not find out what happens if you lose them." The two Boys walked quickly back toward the showers, each trying to look as inconspicuous as possible. "Which line were you in?"

"I don't remember. I was thinking too hard." 62 glanced sideways at 99 and tried to judge if he was a Boy who would report this misstep to one of the Machines. "You know, about tests and stuff."

99 didn't respond right away. Instead, he craned his neck to try to see beyond the identical Boys ahead of them

to the shower stalls. With all the bodies in the way it was hard to tell if any of them had an extra set of clothes in their stall. "I can't see if... wait... there they are!"

62 ran after his brother and they ducked between several lines of Boys waiting their turn to shower and change. They made it to the stall where the pants and tunic lay just as the Boy in the front of the line began to raise his hand to indicate that there was a problem.

"Put your hand down!" 62 shouted as he and 99 both grabbed hold of the other Boy's arm and tugged it back to his side. "Don't tell the Machines about the clothes, they belong to me. I forgot them."

The other Boy, who they could see was Boy 57, looked shocked at the sudden assault. "You forgot them?"

"Yes, he forgot them. Now let's get him changed and you showered before all three of us end up sprayed," barked 99 as he grabbed hold of the clothes and thrust them at 62. He glared at 62 until he started to change his clothes, then pushed 57 toward the Shower Assistant and turned him so that the Machine could scan his chip. Once satisfied that everyone was in their place and doing what they should, 99 turned to the line of Boys waiting their turn. He made a fist and snarled, "And the rest of you, you didn't see anything. If I hear that one of you told the Machines about this, I'll use everything I know about Defense on you!"

Not waiting to find out what 99 might know about Defense, the Boys all nodded their agreement to not tattle. He lowered his fist and now that 62 was changed, grabbed him by the arm and led him toward the exit.

"Thank you for that," 62 said briskly. "I don't even want to think about what might have happened if I'd passed the scanners at the exit in a dirty tunic. Or if the Keepers found out that I'd lost my clothes."

"Don't mention it," said 99. Obviously irritated that he had gotten involved in the mess to begin with he added, "And don't do it again. I'd hate to lose another brother to the Machines just because he forgot to put pants on."

"I was just thinking."

The two Boys walked in silence toward their classroom. They reached the door without being stopped by Transportation Aides and each exhaled the nervous breaths they had been holding.

"You said that you were thinking," 99 said. "What is there to think about? You were just getting dressed. Hardly anything to think about in there other than lifting your arms to make sure your pits get scrubbed."

"I can't tell you." 62 shrugged and looked away.

Both Boys entered the classroom and took their seats. 62 was glad that there were still a few empty desks, which meant that they weren't late yet. 99 looked at him out of the corner of his eye, obviously curious about what was on his brother's mind, but didn't say another word about it.

After the last seat was filled, the door closed, and the tablets began to glow with their pale white light. Man 71 stood and rapped his hand loudly against his desk. "It has come to my attention that there was some trouble in the Dressing Hall this morning."

Both 99 and 62 turned in their seats to glare at 57 with daggers of accusation.

The old Man caught the three Boys assaulting each other with their eyes and cleared his throat. "As I was saying, I was told by sources unknown that there was a bit of confusion this morning. While none of the parties involved made a report of the events..."

57 turned up his hands and opened his eyes wide in exasperation, signifying to the other two that he had stuck to his promise and not made a peep.

"... we would all do well to remember that every action we make, or do not make is seen and recorded by the sensors, Aides, Assistants and other Machines around us. You may think that you can act or react in a certain way and just because a bot doesn't come barreling down the corridor at you, that you haven't been caught. Fortunately, or not, this is not the case." The teacher wrapped his fingers through the heft of his beard and twisted it in a knot before continuing. "Because of this fact, I am pleased to present the first

Behavioral award in this class, which provides the opportunity to tell you about them."

Behind him, digital images of Boys 99 and 57 flashed onto the wall. Below their image their full identification numbers were displayed in large, bold numbers.

"99, you were presented with an unsatisfactory situation and immediately, without prompting, produced your own directive to correct it. For this, you are being awarded the Defensive Leadership Award. This award, along with your current test results, will be saved in your data file and will be considered when the time comes for the Head Machine to assign your career duties."

Beneath 99's photo the words "Defensive Leadership" appeared.

"And then there is Boy 57." Man 71 looked kindly at the exasperated Boy. "In a time of stress, you displayed loyalty and discretion. For this, you are being awarded the Labor Allegiance Award."

Beneath 57's picture, the words "Labor Allegiance" appeared and the Boy sighed, frustration showing in his flushed cheeks.

"Now, don't fret, 57. First, there is nothing wrong with being a Laborer. Without their steady hands, consistent output, and reliability the entire Community would collapse. But just because you receive one award in a category does not mean that is where you will be placed when the time comes. This is just the first of many awards you will earn during your time here." The old Man waved his hands around the room and added, "Yes, there will be a great many awards. Adaline's Head Machine continuously monitors you so that you can be caught in the act of doing good deeds and be rewarded swiftly and appropriately."

The photos and the words projected on the wall faded back into the white background. Each of the Boys' tablets made a slight dinging sound and text filled the previously blank screens.

"Before you, you will find a complete description of the award system. For the remainder of the class, you are to read the description and then select those awards that you are most interested in achieving. Please take special care when you read through the sections that mention the removal of awards." 71's expression became long and tired as he added, "The removal of awards can be very painful and can have very long-lasting effects."

71 returned to his hover chair, swiveled it around so that his back faced the class and didn't utter another word.

The Dream

5

When the tones signaled the end of class, all of the Boys quickly set down their tablets, got up from their desks and formed a line to exit the room. All the Boys, that is, except for 62 who lingered a moment while the drawings on his tablet faded away into the white screen. Once the last line vanished, he set the tablet down and folded his hands in his lap politely, just as he had been taught back in the Nursery.

The Nursery had its own classroom with smaller hover chairs placed in a large circular formation. The Boys were taught to sit with feet flat on the floor and hands folded neatly in their laps while they waited to be called on by a Nanny.

62 waited although he didn't know exactly what he was waiting for. Man 2871 was still sitting in his hover chair facing the far corner of the classroom. All 62 could see of the Man were his two thin legs dangling off the far side of his seat and a sliver of skin atop his bare scalp. After the last of the Boys had been gone for a while, and the sounds of

Boys and Men shuffling down the tunnels to their pods had faded, 62 began to wonder if something was wrong.

Nervousness caused 62's left leg to begin shaking, and without thinking, his toes tapped the hard concrete floor beneath them. He waited just a bit longer and then his anxiety overcame him, and he stood up too quickly, accidentally knocking his tablet off of his desk. 62 tried to dive down and catch it before it hit the floor, but it fell through his fingertips and landed with a slap against the concrete. The noise caused 71 to sit up abruptly and let out a thunderous snort.

71's chair turned toward the source of the noise. The teacher yawned wide and looked over the classroom with an expression of sleepy surprise. Not knowing what to do, 62 abandoned the tablet. First, he stood up as straight as he could, then he fell back into his hover chair and folded his hands in his lap.

"62," Man 71 said in a gravelly voice as he rubbed his face with his hands, "where are your brothers?"

"Class ended, sir." 62 did his best to sit still but his nerves made his toes start tapping again. "I thought I was supposed to stay for the tooting? Or torting? That thing that you said before."

Man 71 rolled his head, neck, and shoulders slowly. He arched his back and stretched his arms as wide as they would reach. "Ah, yes. Tutoring. Certainly not tooting, that is something completely different. I'm not sure that torting is even a word, although I know there are still many words that I have never heard before."

62 was confused by the Man's sleepy eyes. "Sir, were you... asleep?"

"Yes," 71 replied with a sly smile. "Yet, at the same time, no. I was dreaming the most interesting dream. I wish I could tell you, but I'm afraid that I have to keep this one a secret. At least, for a little while."

The old Man winked at 62 with one eye, a gesture that the Boy had never seen before.

"A secret?" 62 began to feel like there was nothing 71 would say that would make any sense. "What's that?"

71 sighed and turned to the blank glowing wall behind him. The second that his back was turned, 62 tried to make the same winking motion with one eye and then the other. 71 had performed it so effortlessly, but 62 wasn't able to make his eyes work the same way. Instead of winking, his face contorted into a mixture of scrunches and grimaces.

"A secret, my dear Boy, is something that you know that no one else knows." He turned around and caught 62 trying to wink.

62 was holding his right eye open with one hand and pushing his left eye closed with the other. The sight made the Man laugh, and he walked across the room to the desk nearest 62 and sat down in the too-small chair.

71 continued. "The only way that someone else might know a secret is if you tell it to them. You must be very careful to whom, or what, you mention your secrets. You never know what they might do with the information."

"I don't understand." 62 abandoned his attempts at winking and folded his hands in his lap again.

"Your drawing, for example. That is a secret. It is something that you do that only you know about. Unless of course, you've told one of your brothers." 71 raised his thick eyebrows. "Have you mentioned your drawing or your dreaming to your brothers?"

"No," 62 whispered. "I didn't want them to think that I am doing something bad. I don't want to be a bad Boy." 62's felt a stirring excitement and he asked eagerly, "Is tutoring a secret?"

71's eyebrows returned to their usual spot on his forehead. He folded his hands under his arms and then lifted his chin to pull his beard out of the tangle. "Tutoring is not a secret, as I had to get permission from the Head Machine to do it. However, what I would like to discuss with you during our hour together is not exactly what I told it we would be working on. So, in that way, the content of our tutoring is a secret."

"I like secrets," 62 decided aloud. "It makes me feel..."

"Different?" 71 asked.

62 nodded. "Different."

"There is much that you have to learn about the values of sameness and difference. Although many Men would not agree with me encouraging it, I am pleased that you enjoy the feeling of difference." 71 pulled his right arm out of its tangle under his beard and as his sleeve fell back, glanced at a small square tablet strapped to his wrist. "Unfortunately, I think my dreaming lasted a little too long. We've only a few minutes left. There is a question that I wanted to ask you. When you dream, what do you see?"

62 sat in silence for a moment and tried to decide how to describe the things that filled his dreams when he lay asleep in his cube. "Usually just shapes and equations from class, numbers and letters that I chase, and playing with my brothers in the Nursery."

"Is that all you see?" 71 leaned forward until he was so close to 62 that their noses almost touched. He whispered quietly, "You can tell me. I will keep your secrets."

The small Boy closed his eyes, breathed in deeply, and held his breath for several seconds before letting it out again. Without opening his eyes, he reached his hands up in the air and said, "A place with no Machines."

The Outburst

6

His first tutoring lesson complete, 62 was escorted down the long tunnel and back to his pod by a Transportation Aide. The Machine repeated the same phrase over and over again.

"This concludes your supplementary lesson... This concludes your supplementary lesson..."

62 ignored the repetitive statement and focused instead on keeping up. The Aide had no concern for 62's short strides and didn't pause when he started to take gasping breaths from the effort. By the time he made it back into his cube with the door shut behind him, he was seeing spots in front of his eyes and his chest burned. He was glad to be back in the small room where he could lie down and rest. He sprawled across the floor, closed his eyes, and did his best to pace his breathing.

Once he was able to open his eyes without seeing spots, and could both inhale and exhale normally, he reached over and pulled his blanket from the cabinet. He adjusted into his favorite sleeping position and pulled the blanket up over his head to block out the light creeping in from across the hall. Sleep came quickly. Rather than the blank and dark emptiness that accompanied most Boys sleep, 62's mind pushed him into vivid dreams.

He found himself in a large room surrounded by thousands of his brothers, all of them answering questions on their test tablets. When he looked down at the tablet in his hands, just one word blinked in and out of the white background.

DISSASSEMBLE

DISSASSEMBLE

DISSASSEMBLE

62 felt the heat build inside of him. It filled his chest until it seemed he would burst and then swept through his body to the ends of his fingers and toes. He felt the boiling inside and heard a loud drumming in his ears.

DISSASSEMBLE

DISSASSEMBLE

DISSASSEMBLE

All of the other Boys in the dream stopped working on their own lengthy problems and turned to look at him. He could see himself from their perspective almost as if he were floating beside himself. His face was flushed and blotchy, red creeping over the skin of his cheeks, and his knuckles turning white as he began hitting his tablet with clenched fists.

DISSASSEMBLE

DISSASSEMBLE

DISSASSEMBLE

His mouth was forced open by the heat and it began to escape him, coming out in a great howl as he rounded on the Machines that now surrounded him. He hit and kicked them, tearing at their gears and smashing their charging panels with his bare hands and feet.

He grabbed at the face of a Keeper and spun it around towards him, looking deep into the whirling gears in its cold mechanical eyes. "WHY?" he yelled.

The Keeper opened its mouth and simply stated, "You've been a very good Boy, 1124562. Welcome to cycle number 3,005. Please make your way to the Dressing Hall and prepare for class."

62 sat up, awake and panting. The bright white glare of the lights above him hurt his eyes. His breakfast lay waiting for him in the food bin, and the sounds of Keepers unlocking doors told him that he'd awoken just in time. He folded his blanket carefully, the heat of his dream still filling his body. As he gently formed creases in the folded blanket, he fought the urge to tear the thin fabric apart. His white knuckles strained with the effort to keep his hands moving calmly.

He couldn't help but grunt as he shut the door on the blanket door a little too hard. To keep from doing anything else that might draw the attention of the Keepers, he swallowed down his breakfast with a swift gulp of the liquid from his drink tube.

Going through the Dressing Hall and moving through the tunnels was a blur to 62. He was so distracted with trying to keep from kicking at the walls and throwing his tablet across the room that he barely completed his test in class before the end tones sounded, and then the heat boiled even more fervently as he thought on how there was no time left to draw.

Again, he waited for the teacher to address him after the last Boy left the room, although this time he wasn't filled with excited anticipation... only boiling heat. He crossed his legs as tightly as he could without losing his balance in the hover chair and shoved his hands under his seat so that the entire weight of his body held them in place.

Once the tunnel outside the class was empty 71 sat next to him and calmly eyed 62's rigid frame. While 62 felt like the roiling energy inside might burst out of him, 71 seemed completely relaxed. He folded his hands behind his head and reclined back as far as the hover chair would allow. "Hello, 62. You've been terribly quiet. Is everything all right?"

"Yes, sir." 62 answered through clenched teeth. His jaw so tight that it felt like it might break if he bit down any harder.

"Are you sure? You don't seem all right. Is there something you'd like to talk about? Perhaps there is some way that I can help?"

"The heat!" 62 exclaimed, his hands breaking free from their position under him and automatically curling into tight fists. He spun the hover chair around with enough force that it lost its balance and bumped into the desk behind him. "What is it with this heat? I can't make it stop. Do you feel it?"

71 nodded silently and leaned forward, kneading his fingers through his thick beard. He closed his eyes, and 62 could see them rolling silently back and forth beneath the thin skin of his eyelids. His eyebrows quivered up and down so slightly that it was hardly noticeable except for the vibration of a few hairs on his brow. At first, 71 seemed to be in deep thought but then his breathing deepened, his head lolling forward until his chin lay against his chest. His arms slowly dropped to his sides as his shoulders relaxed and his spine slouched against his seat.

62's mouth dropped open. The old Man was asleep! He couldn't believe what was happening. He had finally admitted to the teacher his problem after trying to manage it himself, and asked him if he knew what it was, and 71's answer was to simply fall asleep in his hover chair. Thinking about it made the heat flare up hotter than it ever had before, and 62 lost control. Before he knew what he was doing, he lunged forward and grabbed the Man by the shoulders. The chaotic motion knocked 71 out of his comfortable pose and caused both of them to tumble onto the floor.

"What are you doing?" 62 yelled as he shook the broad shoulders of his teacher against the hard floor. 71's only response was a sleepy scowl and a swat of his hands against the small body trying to wake him.

The heat built again, and 62 could feel his skin burning against the insides of his clothes. Without thinking, he got up and stood above the Man and kicked at his legs. "Wake up, you old duster," 62 cursed, "Wake up and tell me what's happening!"

71 finally roused from his sleep with a snort and groggily grabbed at the Boy's flailing legs. "I'm up," he said softly. When 62 didn't cease his kicking he boomed, "Stop it, Boy, I said I'm up!"

62 snapped to his senses at the sound of his teacher's raised voice and sat back down in his hover chair, panting heavily. He unwound his fists, returning his hands to their position beneath him and crossed his legs tightly to keep them from kicking the old Man anymore.

"I'm sorry," 62 whispered, "I didn't mean to. I don't understand what's happening." He could feel the heat drifting away, and his burning cheeks began to cool with the trickling of tears falling across them. "I don't want to be a bad Boy."

71 picked himself up off the floor and examined a scrape on his elbow from the fall against the concrete. "Well, this will take some explaining in the morning when my data is pulled from the scanners. No matter. I'm sorry for making you feel worse, 62, but I was reading my dreams to find answers to help you."

"R-r-reading your d-d-dreams?" 62 stuttered as he fought back the tears that now blurred his vision and wet his cheeks. He sniffled, although was too afraid to release his hands to wipe the tears away.

"Yes. Now this, 62, is a very big secret. You must never tell anyone about this, and never, ever talk to me about it outside the confines of this classroom. Do you understand?"

62 nodded as silently as he could, although his nose kept sniffling as he fought back more tears.

71 sat back down in the chair beside 62, much more gingerly than before, and then leaned close to the Boy so that he could speak in a low whisper. "Dreams can be much more than simple stories and pretty pictures that our minds play for us at night. With enough focus, practice, and patience you can use them to learn. You can solve impossible problems through them, and that is the true reason that I wanted to tutor you."

"Did your dreams teach you anything about the heat?" 62 finally felt safe enough to loosen his left hand, the weaker of the two, from the weight of his body and extend it to wipe the tears from his face.

"Yes. I believe the heat you are feeling is an emotion called anger. It's very rare for a Boy or Man to feel anger because Adaline is filled with the peace and security of repetition and structure. I don't know much about it, but in my dream, I remembered that when I was a Boy, one of my closest and most favorite brothers told me that he felt sensations very similar to what you are describing."

62 brightened at the idea that someone else had felt what he was feeling and that 71 had known him. "Was he able to stop it?"

"No," 71 said softly. "He couldn't."

"What happened to him? Did the Machines spray him and make him fall asleep?"

71 shook his head slowly, tears brimming in his suddenly sorrowful brown eyes. "No, my young brother. Nothing as simple as that. He died."

The Risk

7

"What does it mean to die?"

After the tutoring session when the topic of death arose, 62 spent several cycles trying to forget the sadness in his teacher's eyes. Unfortunately, as with all things, his curiosity was stronger than the feeling that asking this question was a bad idea.

71 covered his eyes with his hands. He pressed his slender fingers hard against his brow and massaged his bushy eyebrows. A soft groan escaped him, and his shoulders slumped, making him seem smaller and frailer than before. He spoke into his palms, his voice muted beneath trembling skin. "I keep forgetting that young minds are filled with so many difficult questions. Why must I be the one with such difficult answers?"

62 wasn't sure if he was supposed to respond or not, so he decided to sit quietly and wait. The longer the pause extended, the more he thought he might not want to know the answer.

Lethargically, 71 lowered his hands and with wet eyes and a trembling lip found the words to answer the Boy. "No one knows for sure what it is to die. All I can tell you is what I saw when it happened to Boy 2783." The Man leaned forward, resting his elbows on his knees and again placed his face in the palms of his hands.

"2783 had been feeling something similar to the heat you describe for many cycles. Every time the feeling came over him it was stronger than the time before. The anger…it consumed him until whenever we spoke, all that he talked about was how he felt like bursting out of his cube and attacking the Keepers. I never knew what made him start to feel that way but once it grabbed a hold of him, he wasn't able to break free of it.

"One morning, we were in line waiting to shower and dress. I was standing a few Boys behind him. I heard him speak harshly to the Shower Assistant. He was saying something about wanting to do it himself, although what he meant I still don't know. Then, he climbed onto the Machine and pulled at the nozzles, banging on it with his fists. None of us knew what to do to help, so we all raised our hands to alert the Keepers that there was a problem. Once a Keeper came, it grabbed him by the ankles. He slipped down the slick metal of the Shower Assistant and fell hard on his back. The fall didn't stop him though, and instead he started to punch and kick at the Keeper, too.

"The Keeper alerted more Keepers to the problem. Three or four more came, pushing us out of the way and crowding the stall where 83 was. All of them grabbed an arm or a leg and pushed him onto the floor. He was screaming; a louder scream than I have ever heard. He told them to get off of him. They pushed in harder and harder until they were all on top of him. And then, the screaming and kicking stopped. When the Keepers pulled away, he lay on the floor perfectly still. He didn't even blink any more. We all waited, but he never moved again."

62 sat stunned, mouth agape. As much as he didn't like the sticky sleep-spray, he had never seen a Machine hurt

a Boy before. He thought about all the times the Nannies had held him close when he was younger and cradled him gently while the singsong of their whirring gears lulled him to sleep. They had always treated him so carefully. Although the Keepers weren't as tender, they too were always gentle when they touched him, their fingertips light on his skin.

"After a while, a group of men from Defense came and picked 83 up to take him away. My brothers asked them why he wasn't moving, and they told us that he died. I asked one of them if they would repair him and bring him back and he told me that sometimes humans can't be repaired. That death is like turning off a switch that can't be turned back on."

The Man shuddered with a ragged and painful sigh, then finally looked up from his hands. The wet stains of tears streaked across puffy cheeks and his eyes were red and swollen. He heaved two more jagged sobs and then wiped his face with his sleeve. He sat for a few moments, and when he finally regained his composure, he smiled faintly at 62.

"Do you think that could happen to me?" 62 tucked his hands back under his thighs and crossed his legs tightly. "Will I become such a bad Boy that I will die, too?"

71 shook his head slightly and folded his arms against his chest, resuming a stance of calm assurance. "Highly improbable. You and I are going to find a way for you to adapt to your anger. As I have said, though I've never seen it done, I do believe that there is a way for you to manage it. I think we should start with your dreams, since you are already having them."

"But in my dreams, I also feel the heat. The anger. Sometimes even more than I do when I'm awake." 62 remembered the dream he had had the night before and began to worry.

"I understand. From my studies of dreamers, I believe this is why Adaline's animators find dreaming to be so dangerous and sought to end Men dreaming long ago. Dreamers see things differently than others do. We are creative, form our own ideas, and feel strongly about the things that happen to us. That's why we must keep our dreams a secret."

"I don't want to dream about anger. I don't want to dream about being bad. Why do I have this anomaly?" 62 asked.

He began to cry, rocking back and forth in his hover chair and looking at the blank tablet on the desk beside him. He thought of the drawings he created while his brothers toiled away at their tests. None of them seemed to want to draw. He hadn't even seen any of them make a mark outside of the spaces reserved for answers. 62 turned to the old Man and sobbed, "I just want to be like all of the other Boys. Without anger, without dreams, without drawing."

The teacher reached out and placed his hand on the Boy's shoulder. 62 was surprised by the warmth radiating from his teacher's skin. It was different from the cold touch of the Keepers. It reminded him of when he would hug and wrestle with his brothers in the Nursery, before they were taught the proper way to behave. It seemed like so long ago, and he was surprised at how much the gentle grasp of his teacher's hand on his shoulder made him miss it.

"My dear, dear Boy. I know that what you are going through is difficult. But I think in time you will find that dreams are a gift. You can do so much more than your brothers because of these talents. Eventually you'll find that you are glad to not be like everyone else."

"Why do you think that?" 62 couldn't think of a time or place when the disorder of his anger, the exhaustion of his dreams, or the distraction of his drawings would possibly be something to be glad about.

The slender fingers of 71's hand squeezed reassuringly against 62's small shoulder. "Because I've seen the spark of intelligence in you and as I told your class shortly after we first met, while we may all look the same on the outside there are vast differences within us. You have a mind, young brother, and I hope that when the time comes you will be prepared to use it."

The Consequence 

8

The cube seemed particularly small as 62 stared at the steel grey walls. Already he missed the few nights when sleep came swiftly to him at the end of the cycle. As he rolled over to find a more comfortable position, he wished that he could forget his tutoring and all of the things that 71 had told him.

He pulled the blanket over his head, hoping that the thin fabric would mute the sounds of his brothers' heavy breathing and dim the haze of blue light that crept in from across the hall. As he lay there, trying his best to block out the peaceful quiet of the night, his anger burned deep within him. Why couldn't he simply drift off to sleep like the rest of them? And what bothered him even more, why did his sleep have to be interrupted by dreams?

He rolled again, this time accidentally brushing one of the sensors on the wall as he grabbed at the blanket. The tiny sensor blinked red, illuminating his hand with the ebb and flow of a cautionary light. He held his breath and lay still, anticipating the Keeper he knew would respond to the indicator.

A Keeper did appear, and he peered at it through faint slits in his eyes as he pretended to sleep. The Keeper leaned close to the wire window on the door and explored the room with its glowing silver eyes. It plugged itself into his cube's data monitoring and sat for a moment, analyzing the information pouring out of the system.

"Are you awake?" The cold, mechanical voice filled his cube through hidden speakers. "Boy 1124562, do you sleep?"

62 lay as still as possible, still holding his breath and doing his best to not twitch or squirm. His lungs burned with the effort of holding his breath in, and he silently begged the Keeper to hurry up and move on. The longer the machine stood there, the more his chest felt like it might explode.

"1124562, you are a good Boy. Goodnight." The monotone voice echoed slightly against the metal walls. 62 strained to hear the Keeper's wheels turn as it moved farther down the pod to check on other Boys.

Once he was sure that the Keeper couldn't possibly hear him, he exhaled and almost choked on the hiss of escaping air. He covered his mouth and nose with the blanket to muffle the sounds of his coughing, careful this time to not brush against the sensor that had just been reset.

The anger took hold of him a little more, and he swallowed hard. He couldn't understand why the anger was coming, or why none of the other Boys seemed to have it boiling through them. This thought, the thought that he was the only one suffering, caused the heat of his resentment to flare more than it had before. Why should he be the only one affected by this anomaly?

62 forced his eyes shut and willed himself to sleep. Eventually, slumber did overtake him, although it was brief and not very restful. In his tossing and turning he accidentally brushed against two more sensors during the night and again had to pretend to be asleep to avoid discipline.

When the slight hum and static of the lights illuminating him from above finally roused him, he found that he was so tired he could barely lift his head off of the floor. He sluggishly put away the blanket, crawled back into the center of the cube and sat cross-legged with his elbows on his knees and his heavy eyes buried in the palms of his hands.

As breakfast came rolling through the tubes and the Keeper returned to download his data, 62 noticed that the Machine was taking longer than normal to tell him he was a good Boy and unlock the door. He looked up at it through the mesh window. The Keeper peered back at him with an almost curious expression. He had never seen any expression on the dull faces of the Keepers before; he didn't even know that a change in their stoic glare was possible.

The Keeper held his gaze for a moment before finally stating, "You look unwell, 1124562. May I assist you?"

62 wasn't sure how to respond to the question and tried to think hard about what the Machine meant by "unwell". He thought he had heard the term somewhere before, but his groggy mind couldn't place the meaning or the context. He peered back at the silvery eyes of the Keeper and finally said, "I don't require assistance now."

"I disagree, Boy 1124562. Your report says that you have only accumulated 4.235 hours of sleep; 47.0625% less than the required amount for optimal functioning. I also read that your sleep was broken up by times of wakefulness. The loss of cumulative sleep function creates a less advantageous position for learning." The Keeper whirred and its arm clicked against the buttons on the panel outside 62's door.

"I recommend a cumulative period of rest to bring you back to full function." As the Keeper spoke, the sticky thick fog of discipline began to seep through the screen that separated the Boy from his mechanical caretaker.

62's heart raced as the fog collected around the door and then began to fill the cube. Without thinking, he reached toward the bin where he had put his blanket just moments before. He had the crumpled blanket halfway out of the bin when the door suddenly snapped shut and he heard a click as it locked. Unable to pry the remainder of the blanket free and becoming surrounded by the fog so completely that he could barely see his hands, he buried his nose and mouth into the bit of fabric held in his weary fingers and did his best to not breathe too deeply.

Although he desperately tried to stay awake, the fog clouded his eyes and he fell, unable to hold himself upright any longer. Just before he lost consciousness, he heard the door to his cube open, felt the cold grasp of the Keeper as it pried the blanket from him, and heard the Machine whisper, "There, there, now be a good Boy and get your sleep. You can resume learning tomorrow, so long as you regain your health."

The Keeper crouched above 62 until its readings indicated that his heartrate and breathing had slowed. Once satisfied that he was no longer awake, the Machine clicked its wheels against the metal floor, left the cube, and locked the door behind it.

62's eyes fluttered open, and the dim blue light from across the pod burned them as if he were looking directly into an electrical arc. He rubbed his gritty eye sockets as a dull throbbing filled his head. The sounds of rest filled his ears and although he couldn't tell just how deep into the night it was, he was aware that he had slept through the previous cycle in its entirety.

"Keeper?" He tentatively whispered through the grate on the door. His call was answered by the familiar clicking of metal wheels. He flinched and squinted painfully as the illuminated eyes of a Keeper peered in through the door. Anger flickered within him, but he found that it gave him enough strength to continue speaking. "Keeper, I need to evacuate. May I please go to the Dressing Hall?"

A screech that made 62 shudder filled the corridor as the Machine shook its head. "It is not permitted for a Boy to wander around the pod outside of scheduled transport."

"Keeper," 62 said a bit louder and firmer than he probably should, "I need to relieve myself. It can't wait until morning. I missed the opportunity to go earlier. Will you please allow me to go to the Dressing Hall?"

Silence filled the space between 62 and the door as the Keeper calculated the appropriate response to the request. Again the Machine shook its head, the un-oiled squelch sending a shock of discomfort through 62.

"It is not permitted." The Keeper began to turn away from the door, and then as if it received some new download of code, it stopped abruptly and said, "You may use the hatch provided in your cube."

As the Keeper rolled away, 62 heard a faint click behind him and turned around to find a door open in the wall that he'd never noticed before. A faint white light peeked out from behind what looked like a miniature version of the urinary receptacle in the Dressing Hall.

62 rolled his eyes in exasperation and muttered to himself, "That would have been helpful to know about the entire time I've been here." He quietly and quickly relieved himself, and as soon as he finished, the receptacle slid quietly back into the wall and disappeared behind a panel.

With nothing left to do but wait for breakfast, 62 lay down once again in the center of the floor and did his best to go back to sleep. Although he had been in a deep sleep from the fog the cycle before, he felt groggy and tired. The pounding in his mind made him anxious to get some real rest. It took time, but sleep did finally find the Boy. No sooner did he succumb to slumber than his dreams took hold.

In his dream, he sat in a vast space with a green floor beneath him and a blue ceiling above him. The ceiling was so high that he couldn't measure how high it was, and the area was so vast that he couldn't see the walls that surrounded him. The green floor below his bare feet was filled with millions of individual green spikes which stood firmly erect but were surprisingly soft against his skin. He turned around in search of the close walls and enclosures that he was so accustomed to when his peering to and fro was interrupted by a soft tickle on his toe. He looked down at his feet and was amazed to see a tiny Machine with six miniature legs marching its way across his foot.

"Welcome, 62. I hope you don't mind the scenery. I get quite tired of being stuck inside C.A.T."

The Boy spun around again, surprised to find his teacher sitting on a hover chair just behind him. "Oh, hello." 62 waved slightly at the familiar figure. "I didn't see you before. I don't normally dream about you, or anything like this."

"Didn't you say that you enjoyed dreaming about a world without Machines?"

"Yes." 62 nodded but also wore a look of confusion. He didn't normally dream about real people and never had anyone in his dream spoken to him like this. It was almost like the teacher was continuing the conversations they had in the tutoring sessions.

"Well, here is a place without a Machine in sight. It is one of my most favorite places to visit in dreams. I call it 'The Meadow'. I haven't ever brought anyone here with me before." The old Man got up from his hover chair, only to get down on his hands and knees on the green floor. He rolled over onto his back where he sprawled out with arms and feet spread as far in opposite directions as they would go.

"I just saw a Machine." 62 pointed at his feet. "It crawled across my foot."

"Ah, that was no Machine. I dreamed up a *Tapinoma Sessile* for you, and this beautiful stuff is no floor. It's called *Poa Pratensis*, and apparently it grows above the Terra instead of being built there. Each individual blade is its own individual organism. I'm not certain how they manage, existing so crowded together like they do. Such a thing seems impossible. Who could even imagine such a thing? But that is the beauty of a dream, isn't it? The impossible exists merely by thinking it does." The Man looked up into the suspicious eyes of the young Boy and patted the patch of green beside him. "Here, give it a try. You'll probably find that you like it a lot better than the metal floor you're sleeping on."

62 mimicked the moves of his elder, first getting on all fours and taking a moment to feel the blades of Poa Pratensis between his fingers. It had a distinct, sweet smell, unlike anything he'd ever smelled before. He took in a big breath, amazed at how enjoyable just the act of breathing in this dream was, and then rolled over onto his back and sank into the thick growth.

The two figures lay in silence for a time, each staring up at the high blue ceiling above them. Suddenly, a thought flashed its way across 62's mind, and he sat up abruptly. "What do you mean *you* dreamed something up? We're in my dream."

The Man smiled cleverly and closed his eyes. "It is true that I am very old, but my age has made me privy to bountiful knowledge. I learned long ago that two people can share the same dream, if both people are so inclined. I've been watching your dreams, and although they are interesting, they are also void of any colorful expression. I decided a place like The Meadow would be much more conducive to a creative conversation than the steel walls of the school that we both already know."

"You've been watching my dreams?" The idea of the teacher watching him was unsettling, especially since 71 might think he was bad. If the Man mentioned it to one of the Keepers, they would probably find 62 worthy of severe punishment. "Can anyone else see them?"

71 propped his head up on his elbow and lazily played with a long blade of the Poa Pratensis. "There are others, and they have seen glimpses of your dreams." He looked quickly up at the Boy and smiled reassuringly. "But they have not seen anything that might damage their opinion of you, and they will not interfere with your dreaming unless you invite them to. I normally wouldn't take over your dreams uninvited either, but I had to make sure that you were alright after you missed class."

62 looked away from the Man as a flicker of anger ignited inside of him. Gradually, the wispy blue that surrounded the landscape darkened until it was a deep red. The dim light around the student and his teacher flickered and created a stark contrast between the red glow of their faces and the shadows dancing around them.

"The Keeper said there was something wrong with me." The Boy grumbled as he tried to remember exactly what the Keeper had said. "It told me that I appeared 'unwell' and that I wasn't performing optimally."

71 picked himself up from where he lay, the lush green Poa Pratensis that had surrounded him quickly dissolving into a floor of black metal panels connected by sharp steel rivets. He crossed his arms, tucking his long beard against his chest and staring at the drastic changes in the landscape.

A row of Keepers appeared on the horizon; each flashing identical yellow eyes as they watched the two figures conversing. 62 turned to face them, and the metal floor surrounding the small child began to bubble and swell as it melted into liquid steel.

"It sprayed me with the fog and put me to sleep for the whole cycle. I missed everything, and it's all the Machine's fault!" 62 broke into a run, heading straight for the line of Keepers. Instead of building up a defensive stance or calling to the Boy to bid him to behave, the dream-Keepers simply stood still and waited for the attack to come.

62 screamed and tears filled his eyes as he pushed the Keepers against one another in a furious rage. He pulled at their hoses and smashed their gauges until they began to hiss and spray fluid and steam. The Boy kicked the Keepers, dented their frames so that they couldn't stand upright, and knocked them down until the group of Keepers lay splayed across the floor, limbs bent at awkward angles.

The young Boy stopped suddenly, realizing for the first time that he could do anything he wanted to the Keepers in his dream. Clenching his fists and closing his eyes tight, he willed the floor beneath the pile of derelict Machines to bubble and boil until it melted into sputtering liquid. As the floor melted, each of the non-moving Keepers slowly sank to the bottom of the boiling pit and soon the whole pile of them was no longer in view. Satisfied, 62 opened his eyes and smiled as he watched the last molten bubble burst. The floor instantly transformed into hardened steel once again.

"I see." 71 spoke softly from across the vacant room. "I understand that you are upset, but you must know that the Keepers and other Machines only have your best interest in mind."

62 spun on his teacher and fumed, "What's that supposed to mean? All they do is tell me to be a good Boy and then attack me whenever I do something out of the routine. They make us all do the same things over and over for no reason, and then if we do anything *different,* they treat us like we have some kind of virus that has to be deleted."

"Yes," the Man nodded in agreement, "that is what they do. It's what they are meant to do. It is what they were designed for."

"They were designed to make me go into a fog-sleep and then not let me out of my cube? Designed to tell me I'm unwell? Why?" The Boy stomped his foot as he shouted the final question at his teacher. The whole room vibrated with the force of his frustration.

"Yes, that is exactly right. They were designed to monitor our wellness and have been directed to take any means necessary to ensure that we remain healthy. Even when it is the opposite of what we feel is right, the Keepers must act if they detect an anomaly because that is their function. It's what they were built and programmed for and is the only function that they are capable of performing from the moment they are built until the moment they are dismantled."

"Who programmed them, then? Who tells them what is good, or bad?"

"My friend, that is one of Adaline's greatest mysteries." The Man closed his eyes and inhaled deeply the smell of sterile steel. When he exhaled, his breath came out in a burst of cold air that cooled the metal landscape created by the Boy. As the heated red and black metal began to fade into polished silver, 71 approached 62 and placed his hands on the Boy's shoulders.

"Dear Brother, until the time comes that you are clever enough to look beyond the steel walls that surround us you must accept them as they are. It will take time, but if you are patient then you will discover your function within Adaline, and hopefully through your dreams you will find your function apart from it, as well. Take care, Brother, and rest. This will be another cycle filled with steep challenges and as the Keeper has told you, you will need to be functioning at your optimal level of performance."

62 closed his eyes as the teacher spoke, focusing on the soft voice and the unyielding grip of the Man's hands on his shoulders. When the silence following his elder's speech overtook him, 62 opened his eyes to the stark flickering lights above him in his cube. The sounds of breakfast hummed through the tubes and 62 realized that a new cycle had begun.

The Failed Escape

10

1124562 was deep in thought as he moved through the Dressing Hall. He was remembering his dream from the night before and marveled at how real it all seemed. He was so engrossed in his thoughts that he didn't notice when 1124999 shouted his number from the line behind him.

"62! Hey, 1124562!" 99 jumped and looked over the dozen or so Boys standing in line between him and his brother. "62, turn around!"

62 continued to slowly shuffle toward the Dressing Hall. It was difficult to identify 62 among the rest of the heads bobbing ahead of him but 99 could just make out the familiar tussle and mess of 62's hair from another night of tossing and turning. 99 almost always found himself in line behind 62 in the morning and noticed that more often than not, his hair was ruffled and knotted.

"62! Pay attention and turn around!" 99 grimaced in frustration and decided to use another tactic. He tapped the shoulder of the Boy in front of him and said, "Hey, can you pass a message up the line for me?"

The Boy in front of 99 turned his head to look over his shoulder. "What is it?"

"62, turn around. That's all. Pass it on, please?"

The Boy tapped the shoulder of the identical Boy in front of him and said, "Hey, pass a message. 62, turn around."

Boy after Boy followed suit, each tapping the shoulder of the Boy in front of him and speaking a message. Finally, after several turns of message passing, 99 saw the Boy behind 62 tap him on the shoulder. 62 turned slightly and listened to the message. A look of confusion filled his face, and 99 watched as he seemed to ask for the message again. 62 looked dumbfounded and said something else to the Boy, who answered by pointing back down the line.

62 looked back at the Boys standing behind him and noticed 99 frantically waving at him. 62 stepped out of line to move back to where 99 stood, when the Boy directly behind him grabbed at his arm.

"Where are you going? We aren't supposed to break the line."

"I just need to go back to see 99. Don't worry, just take my spot. No one will notice." 62 pulled his arm out of his brother's grasp and walked away, leaving the confused Boy to figure out for himself what to do now that there was a gap ahead of him.

"Hey," 62 said as he approached 99. "How did you know?"

"Know what?" 99 stepped backward a pace, knocking into the Boy behind him as he made room for 62 to re-enter the line.

"That I burned the ground," 62 answered. "Well, it was more melting than burning. I guess there isn't much difference. But anyway, how did you know? Were you one of the ones watching?"

99 looked around to make sure that none of the Keepers or Shower Assistants noticed the change in the

Boys' order in line. As he craned his neck back and forth, he asked, "Watched what? How would you burn the ground?"

62 was confused. "The message you sent up the line. They said you told them I burned the ground last night. Did someone tell you that?"

"Oh!" 99 stopped looking at the Keepers, satisfied that they either hadn't noticed or weren't concerned with the switch. "No, I said '62 turn around'. I don't know how they changed that to 'burned the ground. That doesn't even make sense!" 99 laughed.

"Ah, yeah. That is pretty ridiculous." 62 chuckled along with his brother, hoping that no one else had noticed his slip-up. "I guess they lost the message along the line or something. So what did you want?"

99 and 62 each took two steps forward as the line progressed. "I just wanted to talk to you and see how you are doing. Weird things seem to keep happening and a couple of us are worried about you."

"Weird things? Like what?" 62 wondered how much his brother knew. He remembered 71 telling him to be careful not to share his secrets, but worried that the old Man might have told others about his anger and dreams.

"You know, like a few cycles ago when you forgot to get dressed. And then getting the spray and not coming to class." 99 looked at 62 with serious disapproval. "Some Boys never make it back from stuff like that."

"Oh, that." 62 folded his arms and tapped his foot nervously on the hard floor. "Yeah, that was pretty weird, I guess. One of the Keepers told me that I looked unwell. I guess that meant something was wrong with me. But I feel fine now."

99 shook his head and pushed 62 forward lightly to get him to move with the line. "I hope you're fine. I don't think I could stand to lose two brothers at the same time."

62 stopped mid-step, forcing all the Boys behind 99 to stop sharply, too. "Two brothers? What do you mean?"

"1125000 got taken away in the middle of the night." 99 held back a whimper. "He was animated right after me. We were only three seconds apart!"

62 noticed a couple of Keepers coming down the line, asking each of the Boys why they were stopped. 62 turned around to face the front of the line and hurried forward to fill the gap between himself and the Boy ahead of him. 99 realized what was happening and did the same. As the Boys in line behind them moved forward and spaced themselves evenly again, the Keepers lost interest and moved back to their posts on opposite ends of the room.

"What happened?" 62 asked this time without turning around. He listened to 99's answer but was more careful to pay attention and move as he should when the line advanced.

"It was awful!" 99 spoke a little louder than was permitted, and the Boys around them quickly shushed him. 99 looked around and shrugged a halfhearted apology. He turned back to look at the back of 62's head and whispered, *"I mean, it was awful.*

"We were asleep and had been for a long time. It had to have been a long while because I felt almost rested. Anyway, one second I was asleep and the next second there was this screaming coming from somewhere far away. It didn't sound like it was coming from inside one of the cubes. It sounded like it was coming from somewhere farther. Like maybe in the Dressing Hall, or from one of the corridors leading to one of the other pods."

"One of the other pods?" 62 still faced the front of the line, but his eyebrows did a little dance on his forehead. "But we've never heard anything come from any of the other pods before."

"I know!" 99 spoke excitedly, forgetting himself for a moment, flailing his hands above him in exasperation. The Boy behind him bumped him in the back and shushed him again. "Oh, sorry. *I mean, I know!*"

"Even if it came from the Dressing Hall, there's no way that you could have heard it. They close the doors at night, don't they?" 62 took another step toward the Shower Assistant. It was nearly his turn to shower and dress.

"Yes, normally." 99 leaned in close to 62 and whispered in his ear. "But last night none of the doors between our pods or the Dressing Hall closed. I heard some of the Boys talking and they said that they think 1125000 reprogrammed the doors to stay open. They say he tried to escape!"

"Escape?" 62 spun around to look at 99 just as the Boy ahead of him exited the shower. "Escape what?"

99 moved along with 62 as he stepped into the shower and spoke quickly before the Shower Assistant pushed him back out of the stall to wait with the others. "They say 00 was trying to leave C.A.T.!"

The Longing 11

"I understand that there is some talk amongst the Boys in your pod about the alleged exit of a young lad with a knack for programming."

The Boys in the classroom all looked around at their brothers, murmuring and nodding excitedly. The news of 1125000's attempt to leave the facility had spread like a virus. It was obvious that there wasn't a single Boy thinking about anything else. The drone of their whispers filled every corner of C.A.T. and 71 wasn't the only Man struggling to gain the attention of his class this morning.

"Ahem!" 71 stood up from his desk, attempting to look as intimidating as possible. A few Boys in the front row took notice and quieted down, but the effect was lost on the rest of the room. Soon the Boys at the front realized that the rest of the class was ignoring him and resumed their conversations.

71 wasn't one to allow students to rule the precious time he had away from his cube and resolved to take control.

Leaning over his tablet, he tapped his way through a set of commands. And glancing up at the room, a mischievous smile gracing his lips, he selected the final prompt.

Squeals of surprise filled the air, and the din of conversation was overtaken by an orchestra of thuds as all of the desks and hover chairs fell to the floor. The Boys lay sprawled amongst piles of prone furniture, and they wriggled against each other as they tried to untangle themselves from the wreckage.

"There, that's better." 71 sat down in his own hover chair, still gliding in place where it belonged. "If you please, I would enjoy your attention for the rest of our class time."

The Boys turned their heads to face the teacher. A few had been able to get themselves upright, but the majority of them still lay on the floor with heads resting on neighbors, tablets and the occasional overturned desk.

"As I said, there has been some talk this morning about the alleged exit of one of your brothers." 71 tapped his fingers against the screen of his tablet and the furniture around the room slowly rose back to its prescribed height. Each piece of furniture hovered its way back to its assigned row. The Boys silently limped to their seats, folded their hands respectfully in front of them, and turned to face their teacher like good Boys should.

"It's amazing how quickly false information spreads through the Pods, isn't it? I can assure you that whatever you have heard, it is undeniably a rumor with no designs for productive communication."

A swell of murmurs began to overtake the room again, but 71 continued his lecture before he lost control. "This concept of someone attempting to leave C.A.T. is unheard of. There is nothing outside of C.A.T. but the Community, and there is no place for a Boy to enter the Community who has not been placed into a career. If anyone were to try despite those facts, they would quickly find that the code required to attempt an exit is beyond the grasp of anyone in your age group. You are untrained and don't hold the skills necessary for such a feat. The structure of the Community dictates that any action, such as the reprogramming of a door for example, could only be done if that change was approved by someone much more important than any of us. I'm certain that such an approval would not be given to anyone in this facility."

The Boys mulled over the teacher's words for a few minutes in silence before nodding almost unanimously in agreement. 62, although unconscious during the strange event that led to 1125000's disappearance, was uneasy. If he could dream about Poa Pratensis and the tiny black Tapinoma Sessile, who could say what another Boy might be capable of? Maybe 1125000 had been dreaming without knowing what dreams were, and it led him to try to leave the rhythmic life of C.A.T. to find a place with no Machines. 62 raised his hand.

71 ignored the raised hand from the back corner of the room, and instead tapped the screen of his tablet, beginning the series of tests that flashed brightly across the desks throughout the classroom. Each of the Boys began scrolling through the problems without further questions or comments. 62 kept his hand raised high above him, and when there was no response from 71, he tried to reach an inch or two higher just in case his teacher hadn't seen him.

71 turned his chair around to face the wall. 62 lowered his hand to his lap as he watched his teacher's head nod to one side and then the other. 62 knew there was no point in trying to ask any more questions now; his teacher was already asleep.

The Shrinking World

12

62 remained seated as the rest of the class gathered themselves up and shuffled out of the room. 71's back was turned to the class, and the top of his head lolled back and forth with each deep slumbering breath he took. 62 drew his finger across his tablet in silence, drawing an army of tiny Tapinoma Sessile marching across the screen in neat rows.

When the last Boy exited the room, the door slid closed and the sound of the "click" of the lock roused 71 from his sleep. The Man stretched his arms above his head and groaned before turning his chair around to face the almost empty room.

"62, I'm afraid I must inform you that this will be our last tutoring session."

62's expression fell in disappointment as the Tapinoma Sessile faded from his tablet and the Man's words sank in. "Why?"

"A Keeper will be here shortly to take you back to your cube. Unfortunately, the attempt of a young man to exit the pods has made the Community decide to remove some of our more enjoyable liberties."

"I don't understand. I thought you said that an escape was impossible?"

"It is…and isn't." 71 got up from his chair and lumbered across the room, placing his ear upon the door and listening for a moment. "It's my understanding that the young lad did find a way to make it out of the pods, although he soon discovered that there was nowhere else to go. He is being disciplined now, and with any luck will return to his cube soon."

The Man paused and cleared his throat in an attempt to hide a tendril of worry from his voice. "I was told this morning that the Boy is unwell, and the Community is working feverishly to ensure his illness doesn't spread."

"Unwell?" 62 repeated the word that a Keeper had used to describe him before. He still didn't understand the word's meaning. Before he could ask any further questions, the door of the classroom slid open, and a Keeper appeared in the doorway.

"This concludes your tutoring in Coolant Systems and Defense Mechanics. Please return to your regularly scheduled activities." The Keeper held its hand out towards 62 in a tender and reassuring motion, although the pale blue shimmer of its eyes betrayed a lack of sentiment.

As 62 got up from his chair the old teacher moved to stand beside him. Resting his hand across the nape of his neck, 71 walked him toward the open door and the falsely patient Machine.

"Yes, this does end our tutoring for now, but I am sure this will not be the end of your studies. I will continue to see you here in class. Your basic tests are almost complete, and we will begin discussions about placement and duty to the Community soon. Make sure that you pay attention, both in and out of class. There is much to learn so keep your eyes open. Or, shut. Whichever you find to be the most helpful."

71's hand released the Boy's neck, and the teacher nodded at the Machine. "Thank you, Keeper."

The Machine grabbed 62 by the arm and firmly guided him down the tunnel toward the pods. 62 craned his neck in an attempt to catch one last glimpse of his teacher, the motion unbalancing him so that he toppled into the Keeper as it militantly ushered him forward. As he stumbled, 62 saw his teacher turn on his heel and jog in the opposite direction to whatever place he belonged.

"Where do Men live?" 62 asked absently.

"All Boys and Men survive as a part of the Community. The Men live where they are assigned, sorted by career and animation date."

62 had been talking aloud to himself, and the sound of the Machine's response startled him, causing him to stumble again and fall against the Keeper's mechanical arm. The Boy looked up at the Keeper and rephrased his question. "Where are the teacher's pods?"

The Keeper ignored 62's gaze and seemed to quicken its pace. "The information you are asking for is unnecessary given your current training level. Please, continue to your cube."

"How long will it be until I am at a training level where an answer would be necessary?" 62's short legs made it difficult to keep up with the adult-sized Keeper, and his breath quickened with the effort.

"In approximately 1,374 cycles." The unblinking eyes of the Keeper seemed to dull slightly when they exited the tunnel and entered the bright lights of the Dressing Hall.

"Is there a way for me... to accelerate my learning... aside from tutoring?" 62's breaths were irregular from the brisk pace, and it was hard for him to get the question out.

"Acceleration of learning is unnecessary. Please, continue to your cube."

"But how...did…112...5000...learn to...open doors?" 62 struggled to get the words out against the burning in his chest.

"There is no data to support the idea that Boy 125000 acquired training for manual door operation. Acceleration of learning is unnecessary."

62 and his escort approached his pod. When they paused, 62 bent over at the waist and panted, trying to catch his breath. The Keeper touched the data port beside the door and its eyes flashed as it passed instructions to the Community network.

"Is 1125000 unwell?"

"There is no data available regarding the health of 1125000. We have arrived at your cube. Please enter and rest."

62 did as he was told and walked through the open cube door. It slid closed and locked immediately behind him, and the Boy rushed to look through the screen opening before the Keeper departed. "Will he come back to the pod?"

"No." The Keeper's bright eyes flashed with the finality of the statement, and then it turned and wheeled itself away and out of sight.

62 struggled to sleep, turning over again and again as he tried to get comfortable under his thin blanket. He couldn't stop thinking about all that had happened in one short cycle. 1125000's disappearance, the loss of his tutoring lessons, and the odd conversation with the Keeper spun in circles around his mind. He didn't understand any of what was happening, and as sleep attempted to overtake him fragments of the events flashed behind his eyelids.

Once he did sleep his dreams were wrought with sporadic images of open doors, the bright flashing eyes of hundreds of Keepers, and the sounds of his brother suffering torturous discipline. In his mind, 62 ran away from the Keepers in a panic through unlit tunnels and tumbled into endless pits of darkness. Again and again the scenes filled his dreams, causing him to run faster, to stumble over more unseen hazards, and to lose his sense of direction. Each time the dream renewed he told himself that he would gain control and steer his thoughts the way 71 was able to.

Each time he found himself powerless against the decisive repetitions of his subconscious thoughts.

After the dream replayed for the fifth time, 62 noticed a light at the end of one of the tunnels that he hadn't seen before. He ran toward the glowing sphere with arms flailing wildly and hands grasping at the air in front of him. The floor tilted beneath his feet and suddenly he was falling toward the light. The sphere of radiance grew larger and more intense until he was enveloped in its warm glow. He closed his eyes against the brightness, and when he opened them again, he found himself in a shadowy version of the classroom.

Everything appeared as it would normally, save for the gentle prickling of the Poa Pratensis against the bare skin of his feet. He turned toward the front of the classroom and found the familiar visage of his teacher sitting at his desk. Instead of a hover chair, the Man sat in what 62 could only describe as a plume of steam frozen in time.

"Welcome, 62. I trust you don't mind this interruption to your rather unsettling dream."

62 approached his teacher and reached out hesitantly to touch the grey-white mass that 71 reclined so easily into. He anticipated the familiar feeling of hot, wet, burning steam like he had felt when standing too close to the vents in the Dressing Hall. Although the material did certainly feel wet against his outstretched hand, it was cool to the touch and seemed to flow slowly across his skin.

"Ah yes, ingenious, isn't it? I discovered these *Stratocumulus Cumulogenitus* only recently. They are quite delicate and delightful, don't you think?" 71 shifted in his seat, and the entire mass of flowing particles moved to accommodate his new position.

"I'm glad to see you." 62 was distracted as he spoke, his gaze transfixed with the Stratocumulus Cumulogenitus chair as it collected and dissipated all at once.

"And I, you. Here, allow me." 71 closed his eyes and folded his hands neatly in his lap. The walls of the classroom began to retreat into the distance until they could no longer be seen. All that was left was the large blue endless ceiling that had covered them during their last encounter, an infinite expanse of Poa Pratensis, and a second Stratocumulus Cumulogenitus chair. The teacher nodded toward the empty seat, and 62 lowered himself gently into it, amazed that the delicate particles seemed to stay just tensile enough to keep him aloft.

"Much has happened in the last cycle, and I am not quite sure what the Community will do about it this time."

62 forced his gaze away from the shape-shifting chairs and glanced up at his teacher, confusion written on his face. "This time? What do you mean by that?"

The teacher leaned back in his chair, the soft mass beneath him moving as he reclined. "Well, it's never been quite like this before. Similar, but not exactly the same, I suppose. When I mentioned that 00 was unwell, I meant it in an unconventional sense. He doesn't have a cough, and his stomach does not ache. I fear that he may have gone mad. Brilliantly mad."

The student did his best to follow what his elder was saying but felt that the old Man spoke in riddles. "What does that mean?"

71 waved his hand in the air lazily, "You know, mad. Insane. Mentally unstable."

"Unstable? I really don't understand." The cool mist of the Stratocumulus Cumulogenitus brushed the tiny hairs on the back of his neck as he shook his head. It tickled and 62 struggled to not burst out in laughter.

"Oh, there is a name for it, the condition. It escapes me at the moment, claustro-something." The Man lifted his head slightly and opened his eyes just wide enough to view the Boy. "A fear of space, or lack thereof. A very interesting issue, to be sure."

62 tried to grasp what 71 was telling him. He waited for the teacher to expand on the explanation, but when the Man simply laid his head back down to rest on the swirling Cumulogenitus he asked again, "What do you mean?"

71 sat up, visibly irritated that his moment of relaxation was being interrupted by incessant questioning. He closed his eyes again briefly, and a desk with an oddly shaped tablet appeared in front of him. The old Man's delicate fingers touched the edges of the object, and then he opened the top of it like a door to a miniature room.

62 leaned over the printing on the thin screen and read:

Adaline Medical Dictionary
Fifth Edition
Original text authored by V.A. Henderson
Edition editor M. DeBakey

"Have you seen one of these yet? They're amazing, really. No electrical or network connection needed whatsoever. Some of the data is a bit strange, but I suppose anyone looking at something off the Community network shouldn't expect anything less than strange."

"What are those?" 62 asked, pointing to the author and editor.

"Names," 71 answered. "Almost all the people in the books I read have names instead of numbers. A very confusing way of keeping track of individuals, if you ask me. I've looked through countless books for some reasoning behind it, but I've never been able to understand. Can you imagine having ten different Virginias, or a dozen Michaels kept all together? How would you keep them all straight?" 71 laughed, deep and long. His cheeks were red and his smile wide. "Our number designations are much simpler. No matter how many cycles pass, there will only ever be one 2871, and a single 1124562."

A moment later, 71 licked the tip of his own finger, placed it upon the screen and pushed it to the left. The screen curled and he turned it over. Words appeared on the back side of the thin screen as well, and on the screen after that. All of the text seemed to be fixed for some reason, and rather than just swiping his hand across the dull surfaces the teacher continued to flip through them one at a time.

71 looked up and explained. "They call it a book. I've never seen anything like it outside of dreams and wouldn't know how to go about making one. If only the Community knew I had tried! This text and image is affixed to these sheets called pages. Ingenious! The only material I've found to bend like this is the foil that our tablets come wrapped in when they've been out for repair, and I haven't found a way to get words to appear flat and seamless on it."

The man continued talking about the wonders of books, and the follies he had experienced in trying to manufacture one of his own. He continued turning pages as he spoke, occasionally pausing to read a passage that seemed familiar or helpful. After a few moments, the pages stopped turning and the Man pointed down at a paragraph.

"Here's what I was looking for. '*Claustrophobia n. an unwavering fear of enclosed places. Compare agoraphobia. See also phobia.*' Shall we look that up too?" Without waiting for a response from 62, the Man hurried through the pages of the book once again. "'*Phobia n. a pathologically strong fear of an event or thing. Avoiding the feared situation may severely restrict one's life and cause much suffering.*' There's more here, but I think that paints an interesting picture."

62 sat in silence as the teacher read from the page, thinking about 00 and how terrible it must have been for him being confined in his cube. He was glad that he'd never experienced anything like that; although the cube was far less comfortable than the soft warmth of the Nursery had been, it by no means made him feel the need to leave.

"Strange, isn't it? That one Boy out of so many could be affected that way? Well, I imagine that's why the Community has decided to not allow him to return. Well, that and the whole door situation."

62 gasped, "So it is true? He opened the doors to his cube and the pods?"

71 tried to look stern and serious, but a smile crept along the corners of his mouth. "It appears so. Although I can't work out how he did it. I've studied coding extensively

and there is no way that I or any of my peers could have done such a thing. Changing the code of those doors to open is a much different thing than running a system scan and repair."

The two figures sat in silence for a long time, each lost in wonderment of what their brother had done. The table between them slowly faded as their focus drifted away from it, and the Poa Pratensis seemed to lengthen beneath their feet.

"But where was he going?" 62 asked aloud as he thought of the many corridors within C.A.T.

"That is one more mystery I have not been able to figure out. Adaline is closed. You can travel to the ends of it and its walls will keep you from going any farther. But then… what if there were something beyond? A place outside of Adaline altogether?" 71 shook his head and lowered his eyes to the page. "It's a wild theory, and dangerous. I trust you to not to tell anyone I've thought anything might be beyond Adaline's walls."

62 nodded his agreement to keep 71's secret. Besides, who would even listen if he said anything so crazy?

"Regardless, wherever 00 thought he was going, the only place to go beyond C.A.T. is into the Community, and there's no way to survive there without help. If a person doesn't have an assigned place in Adaline, they don't have access to meals to eat, liquid to drink, or any of the other services necessary to live."

No sooner had 71 completed his statement, than both dreamers heard the familiar hum of breakfast rolling through tubes outside of their consciousnesses. The edges of the horizon began to darken, and black spots slowly spread across the landscape like the thick sleep-fog the Keepers dispensed.

"Maybe one of the other Boys will know something about where he was going?" 62 looked nervously at the darkness as it approached.

"Perhaps. Keep your ears open, and your eyes too if you can manage it." The teacher winked at his student. "I shall see you in class shortly."

The rest of the dream dissolved around the Man and Boy just as the breakfast pills fell through the chute into 62's cube.

The Warning 14

Time in the classroom passed slowly while 62 poked his finger at a series of random shapes flashing on his tablet. His mind was rarely focused on the tablet in front of him, but now his thoughts were particularly difficult to reign in.

So much had happened—*was* happening, and the bulk of it appeared to go unnoticed by the rest of the Boys in C.A.T. It amazed 62 that they had already seemed to forget the plight of 00. That morning, when the throng of Boys passed by 00's empty cube on the way to the dressing hall, none of them even glanced in the direction of the dark void of the powered down cube. Excited whispers that dispensed stories of 00's disappearance no longer filled the lines of Boys waiting their turn to shower. It was as if they had forgotten that their brother ever existed or had already severed the emotion that bound them to him.

Doubling 62's sense of anxiety was the knowledge that testing was coming to an end. The easy hours of guessing arbitrary answers to a stream of seemingly unconnected questions were to be replaced with instruction. 62 enjoyed his private talks with 71, but he wasn't looking forward to the long lectures that were sure to come.

62 hoped that class instruction wouldn't be as boring as the training he had in the Nursery. It had been difficult for any of the Boys to sit silently while they listened to Nannies repeat instructions on how to be good.

"A good Boy does not run." A Nanny would say in its mechanical voice.

Each Boy would remain very still, moving only to raise his hand high above his head until the entire room was filled with wavering fingers stretched toward the ceiling.

"Boy 1123856. What must a good Boy not do?"

56 would lower his hand and place it in his lap with its mate, then announce with clear pronunciation, "A good Boy does not run."

The Nanny would repeat the phrase again, as simply as before. "A good Boy does not run. Boy 1123857. What must a good Boy not do?"

57 would lower his hand with the same delicate motion as his brother and repeat with almost identical inflection, "A good Boy does not run."

Again and again the message would be repeated from Nanny to Boy, then from Boy to Nanny until the entire Nursery had had a turn to speak the phrase. The memory of those lessons filled 62 with dread, and made his shoulder twinge wearily as if it, too, remembered hours of holding his arm in the air as he waited to be called on.

62's tablet went blank as the last problem faded. He'd been working on a series of nearly square blocks that fit together to form a bigger block with perfect corners and straight sides. As the mundane image bled into the white background his fingers walked across the screen, leaving small dots behind them like footprints on a wet floor.

His eyes darted from left to right and it was obvious that none of the Boys surrounding him shared his curiosity for what changes were on the horizon. Each Boy held his own variation of the blank stare that permeated classrooms throughout C.A.T. The Boys were so still that were it not for the random tap and swipe of fingers upon the tablets they could almost be mistaken for Machines set on standby.

62 turned his head and pretended to inspect his sleeve. With his face turned down, he strained his eyes to look behind him at 99. Just like the rest of the Boys in the class, 99 looked upon his test in a daze of boredom. 62 suppressed a grin as 99 came to a difficult problem. His brows came together in a knot of concentration, and the tip of his tongue poked out between his pursed lips.

He snorted with a quick burst of laughter and all the eyes of the classroom turned on him. 62 smiled and a slight pink blush crept along his cheeks and neck. Trying his best to act like nothing happened, he tapped at the blank screen on his tablet and pretended to work on the test he had already finished. Eventually each of his brothers returned to their own work and the room resumed the quiet thrum of minds deep in thought.

62 dragged his finger across the screen until lines formed on the tablet, and in a short while he found himself gazing down at a drawing of 99. Pleased with the sketch, he took care to capture the furrowed brow, the tip of his tongue making its escape, and the wisp of brown hair twisted between his fingers as he rested his head on his left hand. The image held for a moment before fading. A second burst of stifled laughter permeated the silence of the room, but this time it didn't come from 62.

71, the noble teacher, was reclining in his hover chair with his tablet held at eye-level. He peered at the tablet, then at 99's corner of the room, then back to the tablet. The Boys in the room looked at their elder in confusion. Only 62 knew what the teacher meant when he said quietly, "Just wonderful. A perfect likeness, indeed."

71 placed his tablet back down on his desk and typed on it frantically. The Boys in the classroom looked around at each other, then each shrugged or shook his head in turn and returned to their work.

X-CURSE

62 looked down at his tablet and noticed words forming on the screen.

"Your drawing has improved much since we discovered your talent. I have enjoyed watching your images form and it saddens me every time I have to erase them. You must be very careful from now on with this talent. The Community is monitoring us more strictly than before, and they may begin monitoring every stroke of the tablet while they attempt to discover the coding issue."

The young artist tried to not let his disappointment show on his face, but when he looked back up and made eye contact with the teacher, he knew that 71 understood how he was feeling. 62's mouth twisted in an attempted smile, and he tapped on the letter keys on the base of the tablet in reply.

"I understand."

Of course, 71 knew the Boy was lying.

The Trap 15

It had been fewer than three class sessions since the last time 62 had drawn anything, and already the heat of anger had returned. He did his best to control it, once again taking to sitting on his hands when they weren't busy with testing and trying to lie perfectly still in his cube at night despite muscles that ached to flail wildly.

His dreams returned to sporadic and violent episodes, and he awoke drenched in sweat and full of rage after nightmares filled with the dismantling of Machines. He was having difficulty keeping his breathing steady and his heart rate level when the Keepers came around to download his data each morning. Every time a Keeper stood outside his cube, he held his breath and hoped none of them would decide that he appeared unwell.

It took an enormous amount of concentration, but for now 62 appeared to be blending in with his brothers. He followed the directions of the Machines, stood in line, and remained silent just like he was supposed to. But the effort to do nothing—to shut down the part of himself that had brought such satisfaction—was taking an unmanageable toll on the Boy.

Rather than focusing on tests like the others, 62 spent most of the time in class doing as little as possible. He tried to keep his toes from tapping the floor. When he had his toes under control, suddenly he had to focus on keeping his legs from bouncing up and down and his bottom from fidgeting across the seat of the hover chair. If his legs obeyed him and his seat remained still, his waist began to wiggle and twist. The determination to keep his waist from moving made him forget his rolling shoulders.

At every turn, it seemed that his body was betraying him. His elbows bent and his arms opened and closed like small doors hung on loose hinges. His left eye twitched while his right ear itched. If he was able to keep everything perfectly still and quiet, just the way it was supposed to be, his hair would tickle the back of his neck, or he would suddenly get the urge to sneeze.

62's nervous agitation was not lost on the teacher, who had tried for three nights to interrupt the Boy's vicious dreams. Had 62 been able to tear his focus away from the burning anger and destruction welling within him, he might have noticed the elder hovering just on the edge of his consciousness. If he could have redirected his gaze from the flickering eyes of the Machines as his hands tore at their wires, he would have seen the teacher waving at him and beckoning him to come enjoy the serenity of his lush haven.

If he could only cease running from imaginary Keepers and stop the drumming of his heart pounding in his ears, he would be able to hear the assurances of his old friend as 71 whispered, "Do not despair, young Man. All will be right soon, you shall see. The Community is changing, and we are not without the power to change with it."

The Leader   16

After seven relentless cycles of battling his own body and mind, 62 entered the classroom to find that it had changed. No longer were the desks aligned in neat little rows. They had been moved into a wide semi-circle so that the center of the floor remained empty.

Several Boys stood along the wall, unsure of where they were supposed to sit now that the accepted order of things was altered. 62 joined them and soon was followed by the remainder of the class.

71 didn't arrive before the tones rang to indicate class had begun, and the Boys whispered amongst themselves when the door closed securely.

"What do we do?"

"Where are we supposed to sit?"

"What happened to our places?"

Irritated that the only thing his brothers noticed was the shuffling of desks, 62 shouted above the whispers. "Has anyone seen our teacher?"

All of the Boys fell silent and shook their heads. 62 threw his hands in the air in frustration. "Well, let's not just stand around here like a bunch of defects. Let's sit down and wait."

"But where do we sit?" 99 frowned as he looked around the room. The desks were devoid of tablets, or anything else that might have an identifier to match each Boy to his assigned seat.

"Does it matter?" 62 walked around the desks and considered sitting at one of the ones toward the back of the room. He'd always wished he had been assigned a seat back there.

"Of course it matters," 1124357 chimed in.

62 folded his arms and looked at the Boys, huddled along one wall. "Fine then. Everyone get in numerical order. The person with the lowest number sits closest to the door, and the person with the highest number will sit near the teacher's desk."

Immediately, each of the Boys sorted out their order, and fell into seats according to 62's plan. In a happy coincidence, 62's desk turned out to be exactly in the center along the back wall of the room and he settled down into the seat to enjoy a much welcome moment of pleasure.

The second the last Boy lowered himself down into his seat, the classroom door slid open, and their teacher appeared. He sprung into the room and clapped his hands. "Congratulations on completing your first group task! And welcome to the next stage of your C.A.T. program."

The Boys looked around at one another in excitement while 71 moved his chair from behind his desk and pushed it to the center of the room. He sat down and beamed at each Boy in turn, his grin widening ever so slightly when he looked at 62.

"In the first stage of C.A.T., we test what you know, automatically, without training. You may think you know nothing, but from the time you are animated you know quite a bit! Well, most of you, anyway." With this he winked at a couple of Boys and their faces flushed with embarrassment while the rest of the class giggled. "Now that we know what you know, we get to find out who you are. Let us begin!"

The Boy nearest the door raised his hand, an expression of confusion clouding his face.

"Yes?" 71 gestured to the Boy with his hand aloft.

"I am 1123856. Or 56, for short."

71 broke into wild laughter at the introduction. He slapped his hand against his knee, and after a moment, wiped a happy tear from his eye.

"No, no. I know your numbers already. That isn't what I mean at all. What I mean is who you are up here." 71 tapped his left temple with his corresponding index finger. "Are you a leader, or a follower? Do you make order out of chaos, or are you an unsystematic mess?"

The teacher looked around the room again, this time with a more critical eye. "What is it that makes each of you tick? Are you going to be a Man of action, or a Man of quiet contemplation?"

None of the Boys had any idea what the teacher was talking about, except 62. He didn't know what kind of Man he might turn out to be, but he hoped that he would become like his teacher. He enjoyed the dreams they shared, as well as the encouragement to draw. 62 especially liked the way that 71 spoke to him, with kind words and no fear of every misstep being reported to The Community.

If he couldn't be like his teacher, 62 didn't know what kind of Man he could ever want to be.

The Good Boy 17

The new format of the classes was much more exciting for the Boys. The entertainment of being able to engage with one another was a welcome change from the monotonous structure they had been used to. Although there still wasn't much interaction between them outside of the classroom, the sound of laughter crept through the dimly lit corridors of the facility for the first time since the Boys' arrival.

The difference in their demeanor was immediate as each Boy crossed the threshold into the small classroom. Rigid shoulders and upright postures curved and leaned as they eased into chairs. Timid voices afraid to speak out of turn had all at once become bolder. No more did each child simply stare at a glowing tablet atop his desk but instead gazed across the room into the cheery brown eyes of his brothers.

62 was so distracted by the enjoyment of his classes, that his anger dulled to a quiet simmer. His dreams remained unmanageable, and he still awoke tired and

lethargic when breakfast was served, but once his eyes opened and he remembered what was ahead of him, the terrors of the night were soon forgotten. The relief from the rage that plagued him left him feeling so light on his feet that he found it easy again to be a good Boy, and he was no longer overwhelmed with the fear of being disciplined by the Keepers.

"You've been a very good Boy, 1124562. Welcome to cycle number 3,201. Please make your way to the Dressing Hall and prepare for class."

62 followed the Keeper's directions with a smile on his lips and greeted 99 in the Dressing Hall as had become their daily ritual. He slapped his brother on the shoulder, light enough for 99 to feel the gesture but not so hard as to draw the attention of the Shower Assistants and Keepers.

"Hello to you, too." 99 turned and smiled before stepping into line in front of 62. "You seem better."

"What do you mean?" 62 asked as the line shuffled forward a step.

"You seem a lot more," 99 hunted for the right word. "More… like everybody else." He nodded and looked over his shoulder at 62. "It's nice."

62 laughed, "It's nice?"

"Yes." 99 responded solemnly. "I don't have to worry about you as much."

"Aw, you don't worry about me." The line moved forward and 62 took the opportunity to push his brother playfully.

"Not anymore, I don't!" 99 crossed his arms and pretended to be offended, but then turned and grinned. "It really is good though, isn't it?"

"I suppose it isn't so bad being like you." 62 rolled his eyes.

The two Boys didn't talk much more as they went through the motions of showering and dressing. Each Boy was preoccupied with his own thoughts. 62 had to admit that the last several cycles had gone much smoother. Getting along with everyone had been easier since he wasn't preoccupied with drawing. He wondered, if he were able to keep fitting in with everyone, would his dreaming stop like everyone else, too?

62 wondered what it might be like to not dream at all. Although he missed the few dreams he'd shared with his teacher, the need to talk to the old Man was fulfilled by their open conversations in class. No more was it just he and the teacher whispering frightening secrets, but instead he enjoyed a flow of ideas and thoughts that he could share with everyone around him.

He nodded again to himself as he decided that he would keep doing his best to be like his brothers. They were all so focused on learning their place within Adaline that they seemed to care about little else. It didn't seem to matter to any of them that they all had the same thoughts and feelings about the Community, or that they all seemed to raise their hand to provide the same answers to the few questions that 71 brought up in class.

Maybe drawing and dreaming had been forcing him to be a bad Boy. Without them, maybe he could simply fall in line with his brothers. Once he'd gotten over the initial sadness of not being able to draw any more, the constant drive to find time to do it and ways to hide it had vanished. It was easier each cycle for him to ignore the surfaces around him, and easier to stop wishing that he had a way to scrawl the images in his mind on them.

As he stepped into the shower and felt the rough brushes of the Shower Assistant against his skin, he imagined that the Machine was washing away all of his dreams. He pretended to watch them fall away, circle the drain between his feet, and disappear into the dark pipes beneath the floor. And then, so that he could be like every other Boy in his pod, he let his imagination pour out of him and flow down the gurgling drain, too.

He left the Dressing Hall feeling like a new Boy—a good Boy. He smiled and followed his brothers down through the tunnels towards the classroom with his hands

by his side and no thoughts in his mind. Just like everyone
else.

The Construct 18

The display at the front of the classroom hadn't been used since testing ended, so 62 was surprised to see the wall behind the teacher's desk glowing when he entered. He took his seat and folded his hands neatly on his desktop as he waited for class to begin.

The stark blank wall cast a strange white illumination across the faces of the Boys. It made their soft, pale skin appear waxy and synthetic. Looking at the faces across the room from him, 62 once again found that the blank stare of his brothers resembled the Machines. He pushed the unsettling comparison aside.

71 entered with his usual flourish as the tones rang and danced across the room with a smile. He picked up his tablet and with a wave of his hand across the screen pushed an image of a large structure onto the wall.

"Can anyone tell me what this is?" 71 looked around the room with a mischievous grin, knowing none of the Boys in the room could possibly know the answer.

When none of the hands in the room raised in response to the question, the teacher walked across the room to where Boy 56 sat. Placing both hands on the Boy's desk, the Man leaned forward and eyed him in mock seriousness. "56, what do you think the image on the wall might be?"

56 looked into the teacher's deep brown eyes, and then up to the wall where the structure shone in black and white. "It looks like… it might be… a box? Something to store parts in?"

Several Boys nodded in agreement and mumbled to one another that they had seen Men carry boxes full of parts and tools when they came to fix malfunctioning Machines.

"No, not a box." 71 shook his head. He pushed away from the desk and stalked across the room. "What do you think, 24? What could that be?"

The particularly quiet Boy gazed up at the picture and noted the small squares that looked like glass partitions dotted across the structure. "It looks like it has lots of eyes. Is it a Machine?"

Two or three of the Boys looked at the scattered bits of glass and agreed, they did look like dozens of eyes.

"Not a Machine." The teacher moved over to stand in front of 98. "And what do you think, my clever little brother?"

"Not a box, not a Machine. Hmm." 98 pressed his chin down against his balled up fist in deep thought. Suddenly his face came alight, and he blurted, "It's flat on top like you could put something on it. Is it a desk?"

71 chuckled and shook his head, the whiskers of his beard wagging against the Boy's desk before he stood upright again. "It's not a desk." The teacher pointed towards 99. "What do you say it is?"

99 was already squinting hard, his face scrunched in concentration. "It has some kind of sign, but I can't see what it says. Is it… a cube?"

The teacher turned, his hands flung high in the air as he shouted, "NOT a cube!" Then he smiled and winked as he said, "But closer. Good thinking."

62 hoped one of the other Boys in the room would get the answer right. He'd only just gotten rid of his imagination, and now he was considering a question that begged for it. He felt a grip of panic seize his stomach as 71 turned to him.

"Surely, you can conclude what this is?" 71 waved his hand over his head, gesturing at the wall behind him.

62 tried not to look at the picture. Instead he stared blankly at the Man for a moment, wishing that 71 were standing a bit closer so that his wide tunic would block out more of the image. Although he did his best to focus on the long beard and smiling face of his teacher, he couldn't help but notice the looming picture spread across the wall behind him.

56 had been right, it did look like a large box. And although he'd never seen a Machine with more than two eyes before, 24's observation of the glass panels did make it look somewhat like it had openings of some kind. It looked a bit like a desk, but it also looked solid and 62 couldn't figure where someone would put his legs if he sat behind it. Besides, the sign that 99 noticed was so small. Whatever it was, it looked like it had to be very large in size.

62 blinked, realizing that he was thinking about the image and not just focusing on the tight crease of his teacher's lips as they curled into a smile. Rather than think about the picture anymore, 62 pushed it from his mind and answered, "I don't know."

71's smile flattened, and he blinked in astonishment. "Are you sure?"

62 made a show of leaning over to look around the Man towards the wall but focused on the desk at the front of the class instead. He paused, then sat back in his chair and folded his hands on his desk. "Yup. I don't know."

"You won't even take a guess like the others? Surely there is something you notice that no one else has?"

62 shook his head and felt both relief that he'd kept his thoughts under control, and shame for disappointing his teacher.

71 frowned, but the scowl vanished as quickly as it came. He spun around on his heel and walked back to the front of the class where he pointed at the picture. "This, my brothers, is Adaline."

Gasps echoed throughout the room, and all of the Boys leaned forward in their desks to get a better look. Even 62 couldn't help but turn all of his attention to the image filling the wall.

71 clapped his hands. He turned to bask in the glow of the black and white photo as if he were also a young Boy viewing it for the first time. "Exciting, isn't it? This is where it all began. Before Adaline grew into the vast world we live in now, it began in this place. A single building where we were first animated, where the first clones toiled away at their duties and laid the groundwork of the Community."

The room became silent as each Boy viewed his world for the first time. 62 noticed that Adaline looked to be made up of thousands, or maybe hundreds of thousands, of blocks each the same length, width and height. The rows of blocks were only broken periodically by glass partitions, and he could almost make out the image of a Man standing behind one of them. The Man held his hand in the air as if he were ready to answer all of the questions running through the minds of every Boy in all of C.A.T.

Two large doors blended in with the front of the structure and once he noticed their faint outline 62 had to work very hard to not wonder where they might lead. To keep his imagination from working too hard he concluded that the doors probably led to the hallways, classrooms and pods that they saw every cycle.

What he tried to *not* wonder was what was on the outside of the doors. It looked so open, with tiny blades of…was that Poa Pratensis on the floor? He rubbed his fingers together absently, remembering the feel of the thin green blades against his skin. The way their cool softness slipped through his dreams. Just like when 71 imagined The Meadow, the ceiling was so high as to seem invisible. A vast expanse above the building. Was this real? Could the things 71 showed him in his dreams exist outside Adaline?

62 pushed back against his chair in astonishment, accidentally causing it to ram hard against the wall behind him. The noise of his collision was enough to pull the attention of the Boys around him away from the photo but 62 didn't notice their stares. Instead, he looked to his teacher.

71 smiled, nodded, and winked.

It was all 62 could do to keep from charging through the mass of Boys ahead of him to get back to his cube. He could hold himself back for a few steps, but the excitement in him couldn't help but force his feet to bound forward every now and again.

"Excuse me," he chimed each time he bumped his elbow into a Boy to his left or right. Every time he clipped the heels of the Boy walking ahead of him, he stammered, "Oops, sorry!"

The Boys surrounding him quickly got tired of being run into and began to move away from 62 as much as they could in the narrow tunnel. Each time a small opening between Boys would appear, 62 would leap forward into a new group and the chimes of "Excuse me" and "Oops!" began again.

When he finally made it to his cube, 62 pushed past the Keeper standing outside the open door. He opened the food chute and swallowed his dinner pills without grabbing for a drink to wash it down. He choked as the dry pills caught in his throat but forced them down with a hard swallow as he pulled his blanket out and lay down on the floor.

Then he did his best to will himself to sleep, even as his brothers were still filing in from their classes and leisurely readying themselves for rest. The slide and click of closing doors, the clatter of pills being pulled from their chutes, and the rustle of hundreds of blankets drilled into 62 and he pressed his hands against his ears to shut them out.

When covering his ears didn't work, 62 forgot his manners and shouted, "Quiet! I'm trying to sleep!" The other Boys were too busy in their own bedtime preparations to notice his demand, although a Keeper approached the door and peered in at him.

"1124562, do you require assistance?"

He looked up at the Machine, startled by the glowing eyes and embarrassed that he had called attention to himself. Propping himself up on his elbow so that he could see the Keeper better, he did his best to appear nonchalant.

"Oh, no. Sorry about that. I was just…"

"Yes?" The Keeper extended its reader into the cube data port.

62 tried to calm his breathing so his readings would look normal. The Machine cocked its mechanical head as if to prompt him to continue with his explanation.

"I was just getting ready for bed. I'm sorry for shouting."

The Keeper completed the download and its bright eyes dulled as it broke the data connection. "Can you be a good Boy?"

"Yes!" 62's reply was a little more excited than it should have been, but he hoped the Machine wouldn't notice.

"Do you require assistance?" The Machine repeated the question more as a matter of protocol than in true concern.

"No, thank you, Keeper." 62 lay down and pulled the blanket over his head. He tried to listen for the Keeper to glide away from the door, but the ruckus of his neighbors was so loud that he couldn't make out the sound. After what felt like an eternity, he pulled the cloth away from his face and peered over the blanket's edge at the door. A sigh of relief followed the realization that the Keeper had gone.

Pleased with his aloneness, 62 once again closed his eyes, determined to go to sleep. The sounds of the other Boys in the pod faded slowly into silence as they each found their way beneath their own blankets.

Because of 62's excitement, he tossed and turned. Every time he closed his eyes, he could see the looming black and white picture of Adaline, as if it were printed on the inside of his eyelids. The Poa Pratensis was barely recognizable in its various shades of grey, although the long individual blades reaching towards the vast open ceiling of the photo gave it away.

He turned over again, shutting his eyes tighter and his mind began to wander towards the image of the Man waving from behind one of the many glass openings. He seemed so small compared to the vast structure; barely recognizable as a Man at all. The Man leaned forward in the image, pressed against the glass like a shadow cast upon the wall. His hand was extended, but 62 couldn't tell if it was raised in greeting, or thrust out in warning.

Now that 62 had seen a photograph of Adaline, he felt a sense of calm. It was like finding a piece to a puzzle that had been scattered through his mind. At the same time, it raised even more questions. He turned again, a little too roughly this time, and brushed against a sensor on the wall near his head.

"Do you need assistance?"

The cold voice startled 62 and he jumped in response. His eyes snapped open, and he looked toward the door with hesitation. "No, Keeper. I'm fine, thank you."

Without waiting for a response, 62 laid back down and pulled the blanket over his head. Although he hoped the

Machine would be satisfied, its voice crept beneath the blanket.

"Your data shows patterns that are elevated above normal for rest, and this is the second time a Keeper has been dispatched to your cube this cycle. Are you unwell?"

The Boy groaned. "I am well, Keeper. I am ready to rest."

"Perhaps I may assist you. Sleep is an important function; necessary for you to be a good Boy." There was a small hiss as the Machine's sleep-gas port opened and it leaned forward to dispense the fog into 62's cube.

"No, thank you." 62 replied as calmly as he could, although his chest ached at the thought of breathing in the fog. "I am able to sleep on my own. I'll call you if I need help."

The Keeper cocked its head in pre-programmed curiosity. "You will call for a Keeper if you require assistance?"

62 leaned up on his elbow so that he could look into the eyes of the Keeper. He hadn't intended to be firm with the Keeper, but its response reminded him of the way 71 was able to instruct Machines. The Keepers and Aides all seemed to listen to the teacher's commands so 62 said forcefully, "Yes. Now leave me to my sleep, please. Your assistance is not needed."

To his surprise the Keeper nodded and moved away from the door, vanishing into the dimly lit pod. 62 stayed there, propped on his elbow, staring out the window into the hall.

He couldn't believe that he'd been able to dismiss the Keeper.

After a while, his elbow began to ache as it pressed against the hard floor. 62 lay his head down flat again and rubbed the sore limb with his other hand. A feeling of power surged through him as he considered the ability to prevent the Keeper from disciplining him. He got a sudden urge to call it back and ask it to do something else to see what it would do. But he was afraid of what might happen, and pressed his hand against his mouth to make sure he didn't utter a word.

Under the pressure of his hand, he smiled to himself and closed his eyes. The image of Adaline shone again from beneath closed lids and 62 imagined that the Man behind the glass smiled, too.

62 felt himself falling into dark slumber. Once wholly asleep, he realized that he was looking at Adaline from the same vantage point as the picture 71 had displayed to the class. The image was flat and grey in front of him, and he turned to see if anything else had appeared.

Steely grey Poa Pratensis sprung up between his toes and expanded to the horizon in all directions. The never-ending ceiling of his dreams with 71 loomed high overhead, but its normal shocking blue color had been replaced by the silver hue of the picture. The landscape stretched beyond the building in all directions, so vast that it seemed to never end.

Turning back to the giant structure, 62 remembered the Man waving out from the glass. He looked to the upper right glass opening and just as he hoped, a Man leaned against the clear pane with his hand extended in the air. The Man was smiling and as 62 watched, he unfroze from his photographic pose and pushed against the pane of glass until it swiveled open in front of him.

"Hello there!" The Man leaned out from the opening and pressed his waist against the dull grey bricks. He shouted across the silent distance between them. "I've been expecting you. Stay put, now. I'll be right down!"

62 stood with his mouth agape as the flat, two-dimensional Man turned and vanished. He jumped with surprise when the screech of metal on metal announced the opening of the left side of the double door. The picture-Man jogged briskly toward him. As the stranger got closer, his edges rounded, and his features became full. It was like watching hydraulic fluid fill a once empty bag, pushing the sides until they bulged and pressed against the seams. Once the Man inflated, 62 recognized him as his teacher and the familiarity made at least one of the knots in his stomach unravel.

"Welcome, my young brother. I was hoping you'd find your way. Isn't this simply astonishing?" 71 slapped 62 on the shoulder before turning to face the picture.

"I don't know." 62 looked at his teacher's profile with amazement, "I guess astonishing is a good word. How did you do that?"

"How did I do what?" 71 waved his hands in the air and a mound of green Poa Pratensis shifted from gray to green. The mound expanded, slowly growing until it reached the height and width he desired. 71 flung himself lightly upon it. The long soft blades bent beneath him and created a comfortable looking lounge chair.

"How were you flat and then not?" 62 wiggled his fingers in front of him and tried to copy his teacher but only succeeded in making a patch of Poa Pratensis turn a putrid shade of brown. He touched his toes to it, and the clump wilted and shriveled into a brittle mess.

71 pointed to the withered blades and they immediately sprung to life, shooting out long and green until they had spread high and wide enough to be used as a chair for the Boy.

X-CURSE

"It's simple dream mechanics. You'll get the hang of it. I was here, thinking about this old picture and wondered what it would be like to take the Father's place in it. He didn't seem to mind the change. Besides, it worked, so that I was here when you arrived."

"The Father?" 62 looked up to the now empty window.

"Oh yes, I forget. The Father, more appropriately, Our Father. He is the one who created all of this." 71 swept his hands in front of himself and gestured toward the vast grayness.

62 frowned.

"You don't understand. It's okay. It took me a long time to wrap my head around the concept. Our Father created Adaline so that we could live in it. Thrive in it. He gave us the Community and the Machines to guide us. And then, he created us from his own body. He gave us the gift of life, and made us brothers, identical in form and health."

62 pinched the bridge of his nose between his fingers as he strained to understand. "So this Man you call our Father made Adaline, and made us?"

"Yes. A tremendous gift that he gave us long ago, far before my time, with a Boy called 001."

"How do you know about the Father?"

"I learned about him as a Boy the same way you are now. When I attended C.A.T. I had a teacher who discovered I could dream, and he brought me here so that I could get to know Father. He had an amazing book filled with wonderful things, like the brown Terra and green Poa Pratensis beneath our feet, the bright white Stratocumulus Cumulogenitus that float without power, and the blue Caelum far above us." As 71 spoke, pockets of color began to creep out from beneath the grey shadows and spread across the landscape until everything around the flat grey structure of Adaline became saturated with vibrant browns, greens, blues and whites.

62 leaned forward. "A book? Like the one we read about being unwell?"

71 shook his head and smiled, "Nothing like that. It was an amazing book filled with words that our Father himself had written long before he created us. My teacher called it 'The Great Journal'. I was only able to read it for a short time before I was placed in training as a teacher, but what I remember of it was amazing."

The Boy's face fell slightly, "You can't just imagine it?"

"No, sadly, I can't. It was so long ago that much of what I read from it has faded from my memory. But I promise to teach you what I know and help you to understand Adaline. I believe that the more you understand, the easier it will be for you to contain your anger. In his writings, Father said that the world was becoming a dangerous place. Other Men were creating weapons to destroy the world as it was. To make it uninhabitable. In his wisdom, Father created Adaline, a place where we could multiply and prosper, peacefully away from danger."

The image of Adaline faded as the Man and Boy began to wake. 62 stared at Adaline intently, doing his best to memorize every block, every pane of glass and every inch of the old structure before it disappeared into the dark. The Man known as the Father reappeared behind the glass with a friendly smile and his arm outstretched. 62 smiled and waved back at the still figure, suddenly filled with a feeling of belonging that he had never felt before.

The Career Path

21

"Where are we?" 99 asked.

The Boys sat again in the classroom gazing up at the bright projection of Adaline, the Father waving down at them from the upper right corner of the picture.

71 turned his back on the Boys and stroked his beard as he considered the question. He exhaled a thin groan and shrugged his shoulders.

"Sadly Boys, I've never seen a true map of Adaline. There have been estimations made by many Boys before you, but the truth is that we do not know the width and breadth of Adaline. This picture was produced when Adaline was first created, and the Community has grown significantly since then." He turned back to the class, arms still crossed under the thickness of his beard.

"Consider this. Adaline began with one Boy who was created during the very first animation ever completed. Now there are hundreds of thousands of us scattered across Adaline in a variety of ages, careers and functions."

62 and the rest of the class looked around the room at one another. 44, 88, and 18 each raised their hand.

"18, what is your question?"

"Where is the first Boy?" 44 and 88 both lowered their hands. 18's question had been the same one floating through the minds of his brothers.

"A wonderful question, indeed. It has been said that after 001 was animated, he became lonely." Several hands shot up around the room and 71 realized his mistake. "Lonely is how you feel when you are apart from your brothers for an extended period of time. It is that feeling of sadness whenever you find yourself alone."

The hands attached to Boys wondering about loneliness dropped and were replaced by 99's raised hand. 71 nodded at the Boy and 99 asked, "001 was made alone?"

71 frowned. "Yes. All alone. The first animation was not a clean and orderly process as it is now. 001 told his creator, our Father, that he was lonely. Together, they developed the process of mass animation so that batches of Boys could be developed and raised together. It is said that 001 expanded the bounds of Adaline far beyond what this picture could hold."

The teacher turned to consider the projection again, and the eyes of the Boys followed his gaze. "This image is merely a representation of where the Community began. Adaline is now so large there is no way for any Man to see it all from one vantage point."

71 touched his hand to the tablet on his desk, and the picture of Adaline's beginning vanished. A second later, it was replaced by a large room filled with lines of Boys sitting at desks and staring toward the camera with the same stoic gaze.

"This is a photograph of boys 002 through 100. As they grew, these Boys divided themselves into several groups with similar abilities, wants, and personalities. These groups fought amongst themselves, each competing for our Father's and 001's attention. Some of the Boys injured one another during the fights, and others stole the food pills and drink from the more passive brothers. It was brutal anarchy."

He touched the screen of his tablet again and the Boys vanished. Three pictures appeared on the screen. The first photograph showed a smaller number of Boys sitting at tables filled with various parts for Machines. Another showed Boys sitting around large tablets filled with blueprints and schematics. The final image depicted a group of Boys standing around the outskirts of an open room, wearing simple grey uniforms and standing at rigid attention.

"Our Father, and his first creation 001, discovered that if they assigned each group of Boys a task then they would cease their fighting and become productive.

"One group was incredibly intelligent, and they were tasked with educating their brothers, planning the expansion of Adaline and creating the Machines to raise and manage future Boys.

"Another group was quite adept at building, maintaining and making theories functional. They were assigned a variety of careers that involved tedious labor and mechanics.

"The final group, those who had previously preyed on their weaker brothers, were taught instead to protect them. They trained tirelessly in defense and combat and used their strength to keep order."

71 touched the screen again and the projection disappeared, leaving the light grey steel of the wall behind it bare. "That is how we came to have three career paths."

The teacher took a few steps and touched the desk of Boy 01. "Education, for who are we if we know nothing?"

He strode again and lightly tapped the desk of Boy 22. "Labor, the noble task of keeping the wheels of Adaline turning."

He moved to the back of the room and touched 99's desk lightly, "And Defense, to keep order so that we might achieve great things."

The tone signaling the end of class rang in the Boys' ears but none of them moved from their seats. All eyes were on the Man as they tried to glean from the twinkle in his eye and the twitch of his whiskers which of the three paths they might be assigned.

62 sat perched on the edge of his hover chair with the same baited curiosity as the brother seated on either side of him. 71 did not look at him though, instead turning his back and walking through the open classroom door and down the hallway.

The Clue 22

After a fitful night devoid of dreams, 62 entered the classroom once again. 71 didn't enter before the classroom bell rang, and when the door slid shut, the Boys sat quietly with their hands folded in their laps. Although all of the students did their best to be good, after several minutes their faces began to twitch, and their bodies began to squirm in a silent display of boredom.

62 wasn't any better at ignoring the urge to fidget than any of the others. Without thinking, he began a competition with 99 to see who could contort their face into the funniest expression. Several Boys around them giggled at their antics and soon the room was filled with the roar of twenty different voices talking out of turn.

Several more Boys joined in the face-making game and 62 was too distracted to notice as 56 got up from his desk next to the door to press his hand against the cold metal sensor beside it. 62 was also too busy to hear his brother ask, "Does anyone know how to open the door?"

75 and 52 also moved to the securely shut door. The two brothers placed their hands on the sensor that their teacher used to open the door, but it did not respond. The three Boys huddled around the panel.

62 was winning the face-making game, and it wasn't until the wild laughter of the group dwindled that he noticed his audience beginning to swarm around the door. 99 stared blankly across the room as 62 realized just how many Boys now had their backs to him. Several of them were pushing their weight against the door panel, which didn't move.

"Let me try," 99 shouted at the group. The Boys opened a path for their brother, and he confidently walked to the sensor and pushed it. Although the action had the same lack of effect as had each previous try, the group again emitted sounds of surprise and disappointment.

62 and the other stragglers got up from their desks and mulled around the outside of the group. They stood on their tiptoes to try and see what was happening. It was difficult to see beyond the bobbing heads and flailing arms, but it was obvious that whatever 62's brothers were trying was not working.

"What's happening in the tunnel?" 62's voice blended in with the dozen other voices chattering nervously. When it was obvious no one had heard him, he shouted, "Hey! Be quiet!"

The two Boys in front of 62 turned around. 12 glared at him. "What are you shouting about?"

62 backed away from the group and waved at 12 and 44 to follow him. They hesitated but eventually broke away from the swarm and joined him a few paces away from the noise.

"Help me get them to stop talking. If we're quiet, maybe we can hear if something is going on out in the tunnel."

The two Boys nodded and then the three of them joined together in shouting, "Hey! Be quiet!" They rushed the group, elbowing the noisiest Boys and repeating their request. Soon the hiss of shushes and the sharp cries of Boys being elbowed in the ribs faded into quietness.

"Who is standing next to the door?" 62 was up on the tips of his toes again trying to distinguish one identical head from another.

"99 and 25 are closest," someone said.

62 gave up standing on his toes and pulled a hover chair over to stand on. From his improved vantage point he said, "Can you hear what's happening in the tunnel?"

Both 99 and 25 pressed their ears against the door. The other Boys also leaned forward and strained their ears to listen.

"I don't hear anything." 99 turned to look up at 62 just as the room went dark and all of the hover chairs collapsed onto the floor.

The room exploded in a roar of surprise and cries of pain as Boys stumbled over each other. The group fanned out blindly, and 62 felt the heavy fall of feet as several disoriented Boys grazed his body splayed out on the floor.

"Ow! Stop moving!" 62 shouted through the darkness when someone fell over him. "Stay where you are! Stop!"

The crash of Boys bumping into desks, fallen hover chairs and each other faded.

"No one move," 62 demanded. He pushed himself up from the floor and gingerly sat up. "Does anyone know what happened?"

"It got dark," someone said. The smart remark was followed by several giggles.

"Does anyone know how to turn on the lights?" 62 barked in irritation. His question was answered by silence as his brothers shook their heads in the dark.

"I have an idea," someone said.

Another disembodied voice asked, "Who are you?"

"I'm 88. Remember that time the teacher shut off all the hover chairs in class? I think he did it on his tablet."

"Who is closest to the teacher's desk?"

"Me," several voices responded. The clunking sound of bodies bumping into walls and furniture sounded.

62 sighed. "Everyone, stay put." He reached his arm out toward the direction the desk should be in. His fingers felt the edge of someone's tunic, and he pulled on it. "Who am I touching?"

"I'm 94," the invisible tunic replied.

"94, get up and go to the teacher's desk. It should be just a few steps from where you are." Bumps and shuffles sounded all around the room. "Only 94. Everyone else stay put."

All the Boys stopped moving, except for 94 whose feet could be heard sliding across the floor. 94 apologized to each Boy he bumped into or stepped on and even apologized to the desk when he ran into it with his thigh. The sounds of skin sliding against metal indicated that 94 was searching the desk for the tablet. It fell to the floor with a crack.

"Ow!" 94's shout surprised his brothers.

A few Boys asked in unison, "What happened?"

"I hit my head on the desk," 94 answered with a whimper. Muffled giggles around the room masked his movement as he searched the floor for the fallen tablet. When his fingers grazed the screen's edge it turned on, shining brightly. It took a moment for his eyes to adjust before he was able to scroll through the commands. He tapped a button on the screen and the lights flickered to life; the chairs and desks resumed their hovering and floated back to their programmed places.

The brothers, scattered in uncomfortable poses throughout the room, shielded their eyes against the harsh lights. The tunnel door swung open and 71 appeared.

"Well done," the teacher applauded. "And with time to spare before the end of the session, too. I dare say that I'm impressed. Most classes don't figure that one out on the first try."

The Stranger 23

62 closed his eyes. The test of the day, a giant puzzle missing three pieces that no one in class had been able to find, left him too exhausted to worry about trying to guide his dreams. He fell into the darkness with reckless abandon, his body fluttering with the dreamy sensation.

The falling feeling slowed until 62 felt like he was gliding through the air. Still surrounded by darkness, he banked casually to his left on a breeze in his mind. The dream, open and devoid of any landscape, filled him with a sense of easy freedom. No walls appeared to contain him; no ceiling or floor to restrict his flight.

His mind wandered and gradually the darkness bloomed into a bright cyan blue, the color of circuits and cables. He smiled with the change and thought for a moment about the intricate network that hid behind every panel in C.A.T. Suddenly, the vast space became littered with giant circuit boards, electrical sparks and hydraulic lines larger than he'd ever seen in real life. He dodged below a low-hanging knot of cables and felt the pliable sheath of the lowest cable brush against his scalp. An outcrop of desks appeared on the horizon, and he rushed toward them. He decided to explore on foot, so he flew in several circles until he found a suitable place to land; then dropped with a hard "thud" on the mountain of furniture.

62 twisted his face in concentration and a portion of the metal desks transformed to soft Terra. He watched as Poa Pratensis sprouted out of the brown mound, quickly coating it in a lush green carpet. He beamed at the change and silently congratulated himself for finally being able to duplicate a heaping mound of Poa Pratensis all on his own.

He lay down flat on the ground and continued to push the Poa Pratensis with his mind. It grew until it waved in the breeze high above him. The weight of the thick greenery caused the blades to bend over in clumps around him. Soon he peered out of a canopy of the long slender material.

62's face scrunched as he focused on a point far away, and then his eyes opened wide in amazement. A group of cables burst open in cascading showers of sparks, the electricity blooming out of its cables in a quiet explosion of white light. He concentrated again and the explosions became measured and rhythmic. The sparks danced across his imagination in time to the beating of his heart.

"Impressive."

62 bolted upright in shock at the voice. Through the thick fingers of Poa Pratensis, he saw a Man lying on the ground not far away. This Man was unfamiliar. He had the same aged appearance as 71, but his beard was short, and his eyes did not twinkle with kindness.

"Wh-who are you?"

The Man rolled onto his side and wiped a broken blade of Poa Pratensis from his tunic. He sighed. "Does it really matter? In the end we are the same cog in the same giant wheel. Always turning but never changing, each generation following the footsteps of the one before without deviation."

62 ducked back into the protection of the bushy growth surrounding him. He held his breath, hoping that the Man was just a part of his dream and that he'd disappear if he thought hard enough about something else.

Before 62 could refocus though, the long blades that shielded him began to shorten. Inch by inch they disappeared, receding back into the Terra and exposing the stranger again.

"Oh, please don't bother trying to hide. My mind is much more powerful than yours and I'd rather not have to go on some wild imaginative chase through your silly dream." The Man got up from where he lay, smoothed his tunic until every crease was straight, and then tapped his foot against the mountain of desks. Immediately, the entire scene vanished and was replaced by a small red room with a single naked light bulb dangling from the ceiling. The swinging light cast odd shadows about the room making the Man's appearance shift unnaturally.

62 got up from the floor. As he stood, his body was forced down by invisible hands into a simple black hover chair. The chair dragged itself a few feet toward the center of the room, and 62 found himself seated directly below the bare bulb.

"What is this place?" 62 uttered finally.

"This is my room. I call it the Hall of Questions. Delightful, isn't it?" The Man snapped his slender fingers together and a high-backed hover chair appeared in the corner of the room. The Man eased into it and rubbed the palm of his hands together. When he opened them again, a small tablet appeared. He began reading it silently.

"The Hall of Questions?" 62 fidgeted in his seat.

"Yes. Mine though, not yours." The stranger's hand glided across the tablet, and he paused for a moment, something on the screen catching his interest. "So the question really is, who are you?"

"I am Boy 1124562. I am currently assigned to the Career Aptitude Testing Compound and awaiting my career assignment." 62 spoke his response obediently and mechanically, as he had been trained to do from the time he was able to talk.

"Really. Well that's certainly interesting." The Man reclined farther into his seat, the edges of the chair casting shadows across his face so that 62 could no longer read his expression. "And how long have you been able to dream?"

Although he'd been taught to always respond truthfully and completely to any question posed to him, something about this stranger made 62 feel uneasy. He thought back for a moment to the conversation he had with 71 early in their tutoring when the teacher had warned him to be wary of others knowing about his ability.

"This is my first time, sir. I think. Is this a dream?"

The Man grinned, the curl of his lips barely visible in the dark shadows. "As I said, this is a room for my questions, Boy. Please keep yours to yourself. Are you quite sure this is your first time using your imagination?"

62 lied again. "I don't know what imagination is, sir. I don't think I have been given that device."

The Man leaned forward in his chair. His expression was supposed to look kind, but 62 could see that his friendliness wasn't genuine. "But then where did the grass and fireworks display come from?"

62 didn't have to pretend to be baffled by the question and responded earnestly. "I'm sorry, sir. I don't know what grass or fireworks are."

The intense stare that 62 received in response to his answer made him worry that he had said something wrong. He fought the urge to expand on his answer, afraid that if he opened his mouth, he would let loose some information that the stranger would use against him. 62's muscles tightened as the tension in the room seemed to swell around him.

62 started to think that maybe he could stand up from the chair, slap himself in the face, and force himself to wake up. Dreams, after all, can't really hurt the dreamer. But then he remembered that 71 was able to see into his dreams, and the teacher had said other Men could view his dreams also. 62 worried that if he showed he knew how to wake himself

up, the Man would know he was lying about this being his first dream.

"Are you quite sure that this is your first dream, and that you are not responsible for the grass or the fireworks?"

62 jumped slightly as the question broke the silence and then nodded.

"Hmm. That is also very interesting. It's also a very good thing, for you." The Man got up from his chair and it vanished. The tight walls began to expand outward, and the eerie light bulb expanded into a large bright light high above them.

"This dream that you are having is an anomaly. It is not a normal function of your brain and could be a sign of being unwell. Good Boys do not dream. Do you understand?" The Man again tried to look friendly, but something in his eyes still frightened 62.

"I want to be a good Boy." 62 replied in the exact tone and rhythm that he had been taught as far back as he could remember. "Good Boys do not dream."

"If you continue to experience these anomalies, you are to report them to the nearest Keeper so that the issue may be corrected. Do you understand?" The Man put his hand on 62's shoulder, mimicking the reassuring gesture that 71 used so frequently.

62 fought a flinch of discomfort from being touched by the stranger and nodded. "Good Boys always report anomalies to their Keeper."

The strange Man leaned down until his eyes were level with 62's. He let go of his mask of friendliness and spoke sharply. "If you experience this anomaly again and do not report it, you will be disciplined in any manner that I see fit. Believe me when I say that you do not want to experience my discipline. I will do things to you far worse than make you take a little nap in your cube."

62 couldn't help but gasp. He already knew he did not want to ignore this Man's warning.

"Now, wake up." A hole appeared in front of 62 and the Man pushed him into it.

62 sat up, suddenly awake in the dark of his cube. He could hear his brothers still sleeping around him and glanced out into the empty hall. He panted and put his hand over his chest, which felt like it might burst open from the panicked racing of his heart.

Somehow, he could hear the voice of the dream-Man echo through his mind. "And don't tell anyone what you just saw."

The Anomaly 24

It had been several cycles since the strange Man entered his dream, but his warning still rang in 62's ears. As his brothers slept, 62 lay awake, staring at the ceiling of his pod, once again afraid to fall asleep. He didn't know what to do about the Man, or his dreams.

The last few classes had passed by in a blur, with 62 spending most of his time trying to send signals to 71 that he needed help. He raised his hand often during class to try and ask the teacher questions that might catch his attention, but 71 never seemed to notice.

When he couldn't get the teacher's attention, 62 decided to try and talk to 71 after class. No matter how quickly 62 sprung from his chair, the teacher seemed to vanish into the tunnels the second the bell rang. 62 felt that his teacher was avoiding him. The lack of attention was so severe that even some of the other Boys had noticed the change.

"What did you do to make the teacher stop calling on you all of a sudden?" 99 asked as they were walking back to the pod after class.

"I don't know." 62 shrugged and shook his head in confusion. "One cycle he tells me I did a good job making decisions solving those crazy tests, and then the next cycle it's like I don't exist. I don't know what I did."

"Well you'd better figure it out soon. Some of our brothers are starting to talk about you being bad or something." 99 added before ducking into his cube, "Some of us are afraid you're going to be disciplined soon."

Thinking back on the conversation later that night didn't help 62 relax any, and he rolled over on the floor. He was so tired that his eyes burned, and he could barely hold his eyelids open. He didn't want to be disciplined, not by the Keepers, and certainly not by the strange Man in his dream. Maybe he *had* been bad, and just didn't know it.

He pressed the heels of his hands against his dry eyes and could almost feel the irises crack under the pressure. Releasing them, he blinked furiously before being overtaken by a yawn. If he could only stay awake one more night, maybe he could figure out what to do tomorrow…

"Come back, brother."

62's vision blurred. He saw two long, dark tunnels and then tiny slits before he was consumed by the darkness.

"1124562, come back to sleep."

A face started to form in the darkness ahead of him. It was a copy of every Man 62 had ever encountered. Two brown eyes shown from under grey brows, and a beard started to form around the Man's face.

62's eyes snapped open as he realized he had fallen asleep. He slapped his face and sat up in his cube, careful not to touch the sensors. He couldn't believe he'd let himself fall asleep like that – or that a face had formed so quickly. But who was it? 62 hadn't gone deep enough into the dream to tell if it was his teacher, the unfriendly stranger, or someone else.

X-CURSE

He shook his head to try to clear the drowsiness but only succeeded in making himself lightheaded and dizzy. He lay down again to keep from falling against the wall of the cube, and held his eyelids open with his fingers.

"Good Boys do not dream," he mumbled.

He yawned so deeply that his muscles shook beneath his tunic and his trembling fingers lost their grip on his eyelids. They snapped shut in an uncontrolled blink and it was all that 62 could do to pry them open again.

"Good Boys do not dream," he repeated.

"Not all good Boys dream. But you do, and you're a good Boy."

62 couldn't tell where the voice he heard was coming from and then realized that the words were ringing in his ears. "Come back, brother. Come back to your dreams."

"Good Boys do not dream!" 62 shouted, pushing the unknown voice from his head. He reached out and touched the sensor on the wall and waited for a Keeper to come to the door.

"Boy 1124562, do you require assistance?"

"Yes, Keeper." 62 crawled over to the door and looked up at the Machine's glowing blue eyes. "I am experiencing an anomaly."

The Elevator 25

The sign across the hall didn't have time to scroll through its data three times before 62 was brought out of his cube under the watchful gaze of Machines. The two Transportation Aides in charge of his removal were gentle with him as they laid him on a stiff board bolted to a pushcart. They waited for him to get comfortable before covering him up with a fresh blanket.

Neither Aide spoke and 62 was too afraid to break the silence as they pushed him toward a wall in the tunnel. The seamless panel ahead of them split in two, a bright white light filling the cracks and creases of a hidden door. Two side panels slid open silently, allowing enough room for both Aides and the cart 62 lay on to pass easily into the secret hallway.

62 stared up and counted the number of fluorescent lights on the narrow ceiling as the Aides pushed him. "One… Two… Three… Four…"

Neither Aide responded to the sound of his voice. Both Machines kept their glowing eyes faced forward and continued pushing the gurney down the long, stark hallway.

"Eleven… Twelve… Thirteen…"

Large panels separated the fluorescent lights. 62 noticed they were made of a different material than the hard steel surfaces in C.A.T. The material appeared to have once been painted white, but the corners of each tile had become yellow with age. In some areas the ceiling had been discolored by large brown spots, and they reminded 62 of an upside-down oil spill.

"Twenty-eight, Twenty-nine, Thirty…"

It seemed the hallway would never end. 62 counted all the way to one hundred and seven before losing track of the numbers. He craned his head to look around the Aide pushing the cart near his head and was amazed at how far away from the pods they had traveled. He turned again to look past the Aide pulling the gurney down at his feet and could only just barely make out a small metal door at the end of the hall. He glanced around and noticed that no other doors lined the walls of the hallway. Every once in a while, a picture of a Machine, a group of Boys, or a Man hung on the wall but otherwise the hallway was devoid of decoration.

The trio reached the end of the hallway and the Aide near 62's feet reached over to the right side of the metal door to push one of only two buttons on the wall. As its mechanical finger released the button, a green ring glowed around it and an arrow pointing toward the ceiling illuminated. The other button, mounted directly below it, remained unlit.

62 looked up at the two Aides looming over him. They appeared to be waiting for something to happen. The green circle around the up arrow persisted, and there was no other change in the hallway. 62 raised his head up off of the cart to get a better view. They waited, and waited, and waited some more but nothing seemed to change.

"I think the door is broken." 62 looked up at one of the Aides, and then the other for a response. Neither Machine paid him any attention.

He cautiously sat upright on the gurney, and leaned forward to get a better look at the door. As was typical in C.A.T., the door had no handle and appeared to sink into the wall with no way of pulling or pushing it open. 62 scooted toward the foot end of the cart, leaned carefully around the Travel Aide at the foot of the gurney and pressed the up-arrow button again.

Still nothing happened, aside from a tiny "click" that sounded in the panel as 62 pressed and depressed the round button. The green light stayed illuminated. He pressed it again, and then a moment later tapped it four or five times. When nothing happened, he pressed the button below it. The down arrow illuminated, a circle of red light surrounding it. Aside from the additional illumination of the second button, nothing else happened.

"Call a repair Man to come and fix this thing. It's broken." 62 did his best to command the two Transportation Aides who seemed to not notice him. Bored and frustrated, 62 slid his legs off the gurney and considered dropping off the cart onto the floor.

"Remain on your transportation device." Both Aides spoke the direction in unison.

"The door's broken. Nothing is happening. I'm going to see if I can fix the buttons." 62's toes reached out toward the floor.

Instantly, one of the Transportation Aides grabbed at his shoulders, the other took his knees. They lifted him up and placed him back onto the gurney. Their mechanical hands pushed him down until he was again lying flat, and one of them straightened the crumpled blanket and covered him with it again.

"Please remain lying down for the duration of your transport. Keep your arms and legs inside the gurney at all times. Failure to obey may result in accidental injury." The two voices spoke as one.

The metal door ahead of them slid open and the two Aides pushed 62 through the opening into a small metal room. There was just enough space for the two Machines and the gurney in the little box. The door slid closed behind them.

The Aide near 62's head reached over to the panel on the right side of the door. Hundreds of tiny buttons filled the panel. The Machine pushed a button with the number "2" printed on it. A digital readout above the door illuminated the number "B32".

"Going up," a small mechanical voice announced.

A moment later the box began to move. The vertical movement was disorienting and 62 focused on the numbers flashing above the door to distract himself from the anxious fear creeping into his mind.

"B32… B31… B30… B29…"

The numbers flashed to B01, and then L1, and then rested at the number 2. The metallic door opened again with a screech.

62 was pushed out of the little box and into another hallway. He began to think that maybe reporting his dream anomaly hadn't been such a good idea.

The Doctor 26

62 lay on a white bed covered with a stiff plastic sheet. The room he had been taken to was simple. It was similar to the starkness of a cube aside from its large size and the presence of furniture. Not only was there room for the bed he now occupied, but also for three Keepers to stand at a comfortable distance around him.

Intimidated by his companions, 62 lay stiff and silent. The rise and fall of his breathing moved his torso enough to make the sheet below crackle. The Keepers stood unmoving and emotionless as if they, too, were waiting for something ominous to happen.

After what seemed like several cycles, the blue metal door to his left opened. A Man strode through wearing a long white coat over his tunic, his attention firmly affixed to a large tablet in his hands. Without looking up the Man said, "Good cycle, Keepers."

The three Keepers' eyes flashed blue, and they responded, "Good cycle, Doctor."

The Man set his tablet on a thin white table in the far corner of the room, sat down on a simple white hover chair, and propelled himself toward the bed. "And who do we have here?"

62 immediately recognized the Man. The false smile, the short and meticulously groomed beard, and the cold look in his eyes was the same as the stranger from 62's dream. The Man didn't appear to recognize him.

"This is Boy 1124562, Doctor." The Keeper to 62's left put its hand down on his arm and pressed it to the mattress.

"Oh?" The doctor's eyes flashed with interest. He raised an eyebrow and leaned in to look at 62. "And what is the complaint?"

"Anomaly of cognition." The Keeper to 62's right put its hand down on his other arm and pressed it to the mattress with a force equal to its mate.

"Voluntary surrender, or disciplinary action?" The doctor pulled a pair of white gloves over his thin hands, snapping the taut material against his skin. He leaned over 62's head and pulled at the Boy's eyelids to examine his eyes.

"Voluntary. Approximately 0.26 cycles ago." The third Keeper placed both of its hands on 62's ankles and pushed down as well.

"Very good." The doctor nodded his approval.

62 was relieved when the doctor let go of his eyelids. The examination was far from complete though and soon the gloved hands were examining the contours of his hairline. The long fingers circled his temples, then pushed along his jaw line deep beneath the skin.

"No signs of trauma to the brain. No swelling or abnormal growth beneath the skin." The doctor pressed firmly against 62's throat and the unusually strong but tender fingers touched every muscle and tendon all the way down to the Boy's upper chest. "Vitals?"

"Slightly elevated, likely due to stress." The chest on the Keeper to 62's right flashed bright blue and a screen showing various charts, graphs and a picture of a beating heart appeared.

The doctor watched the Keeper's display for a moment as his hands moved down and then back up each of 62's arms. He moved his skilled hands down 62's chest, touching every rib before pressing into the soft flesh of his abdomen.

"Likelihood of recovery from the procedure to correct the anomaly?"

"Unknown." The Keeper to 62's left turned on its display as well and text slowly scrolled across the screen. "Should the patient recover, likely side effects will be confusion, sustained retrograde and anterograde memory loss, muscle pain, broken bones, and mild cognitive damage."

"And should the patient not recover?" The doctor's face twitched into a temporary smile.

"An acceptable percentage of patients treated with Electroconvulsive therapy experience reoccurrence of anomalies, uncontrolled seizure, or death." The Keeper at 62's feet turned on a third screen which slowly scrolled through photographs of Boys in various states of medical distress.

62 studied each of the screens as the doctor and Keepers carried out their conversation. His heart thumped hard against his chest, and he could feel the sweat dripping from his forehead. He pulled his arms and legs under the force of the Keeper's hands and realized that there was no way to escape.

"What are you going to do to me?" 62's voice cracked.

The doctor, intent on reviewing the screen displaying grisly photos of patients, did not look at 62 when he spoke. Matter-of-factly he replied, "We're going to attempt to repair you. Your central nervous system is malfunctioning when you enter rest state. We are going to pass a current of electricity through your brain; essentially reprogramming it to function in the manner it was intended."

"I don't want electricity in my brain." 62 had to look away from a picture of a Boy whose bones had broken through the skin in several places over his body. "I promise not to have anomalies anymore."

The doctor laughed. "No one ever wants to find out what it's like to be reset. I promise you: once the procedure is complete you won't remember a thing."

Despite 62's protest, the doctor began to scurry around the room preparing himself and gathering his instruments for the procedure. He asked 62 to open his mouth wide, and when the Boy obeyed, pushed a hard rubber tube between his teeth. The tube pressed against his tongue, forcing him to gag. Bile rose up from his stomach and burned his throat, but the tube that filled his mouth prevented it from going any farther. He swallowed hard, forcing it back down. As his head thrashed from side to side, one of the Keepers wrapped a cold metal band around it and ratcheted him down to the bed.

"Struggling will only make this worse." The doctor grinned with malevolence as he and the Keepers used more metal bands to strap him to the bed. Across his chest, waist, wrists, hips, thighs and calves went the straps. Each was affixed firmly to rails at the side of the bed.

The band pressed into 62's forehead had two thick bumps that pressed into his skin. To these, the doctor attached two long wires that ran alongside the bed and connected to a large white box with several dials and primitive displays.

From the corner of his eye, 62 could see the doctor turn on the contraption and bring the needles on the display bouncing to life. He tested the dials, making the needles on the gauges jump from left to right.

"Electrodes are ready, Doctor." One of the three Keepers held two black wands out toward the doctor while another Keeper plugged their attached cables securely into the box.

Once again, the doctor sat at 62's head and motioned for the Keeper with the electrode wands to bring them to him. It leaned across the short space and handed them to him carefully.

The wands, held in the experienced hands of the doctor, were pressed against 62's temples. 62 cried. He tried to beg the doctor to stop but the hard rubber in his mouth only allowed a few grunts to escape.

"Keeper, please begin the treatment." The doctor smiled.

The Keeper's hand had just twitched toward the dial on the box with wires connected to 62's head when there was a loud rustling outside of the room. The doctor and the Keepers each turned their heads toward the door. 62's head refused to turn under the pressure of the straps holding his head to the bed, so he peered through watery eyes as far toward the sounds as he could.

A Man yelled something unintelligible from outside and then there was a quick procession of thuds against the heavy metal door. As abruptly as the disturbance started, it stopped, and the room was again filled with silence.

"Keeper, I demand you proceed." The doctor's voice shook in frustration. His thin fingers gripped the wands against 62's head so tightly that his knuckles turned white.

"Beginning therapy session number one," the first Keeper said as it leaned toward the dials once more. Its fingers touched the large switch in the center of the contraption.

The blue metal door swung open with a loud screech and a clang. For once, 62 was glad that the Machines did not react to sudden movements and sounds the way Boys and Men did. Instead of startling with the sudden intrusion of another Man into the room, the Keeper simply paused and stood frozen in time waiting for its next command.

"Stop this madness!" The Man rushed the small group and began pulling at the restraints holding 62 tight.

62 looked up through a well of tears to see 71 unceremoniously pulling at the straps. He tried to shout out his recognition, but the noise that passed through the hard

rubber wedged between his teeth and over his tongue came out as a garbled "Uaaaghhh!"

The doctor stood up from his hover chair with such quickness that it skidded across the room and crashed into the thin table against the wall. "What are you doing? We're in the middle of a procedure!"

62's head, arms and legs were suddenly covered in a flurry of moving hands. 71 raced around undoing the restraints to pull 62 from the table, and the doctor rushed behind just as quickly re-fastening the straps.

"The proper steps were not followed to authorize this treatment." 71 stumbled as he spoke, already out of breath from his endeavors.

"The patient came to us voluntarily, complaining of an anomaly. No further steps were necessary." The doctor wheezed back to his similarly aged brother.

"He's just a Boy. Unable to assess his own behaviors. You know that in these cases a teacher must be notified of his student's perceived conditions!" 71 scraped 62's arm as he tried to release it again from its confines.

The doctor raged. "You were informed, obviously, for here you are!" He grabbed the same arm 71 was trying to free and shoved it back against the bed.

71 let go of the strap he had been loosening and grabbed the doctor's coat instead. The doctor grasped at 71's long beard and the two pushed and pulled themselves across the room, knocking into the bed, Keepers and tables as they struggled against one another.

"Doctor. Man 2871. Cease your assault." All three Keepers chimed with the same unified voice. Their eyes all began to glow blue, and their sleep fog ports opened in their chests.

The two Men froze in their struggle with one another. They each looked toward the Keeper closest to them and slowly let go of their brother. The Men separated by two full paces, and each straightened his garments and cleared his throat respectfully.

71 spoke again, and although his message was directed toward the doctor, he did not break his gaze with the Keeper beside him. "Doctor, it has been brought to my attention that the patient is below the allowable age for voluntary surrender. As his assigned teacher, I am responsible for monitoring any perceived anomalies and filing a formal report prior to attempted treatment."

The doctor stood up straight and walked past the Keepers back toward the table. "The approval for the procedure has already been given. It must proceed."

71's jaw tensed and he spoke now to the Machines. "Keeper, have all procedures and requirements been met for the treatment of Boy 1124562?"

All three Keepers' eyes flashed blue as they reviewed the record in their systems. The Keeper standing closest to 62's bed replied, "Negative. Proper reporting of the procedure by the Boy's authoritative figure has not been filed. The procedure was approved by administrative staff without a signature. Teacher 2871, do you verbally approve this procedure for your student?"

"I do not." 71 stated through gritted teeth.

"Voluntary surrender is void in cases which involve Boys where documentation is not complete." The Keeper began to undo all of the restraints holding 62 to the bed. A second Keeper removed the electrodes from his temples and put the electrical wands back on their table. The third Keeper removed the hard block of rubber from between his teeth and put it in a sanitation tray in the corner.

"Well, that settles that, then." 71 took 62 by the hand and pulled him gingerly off the bed. "Keeper, will you kindly bandage 62's arm? That is quite the scratch he has there."

One of the Keepers gingerly cleaned 62's arm and covered it with a strip of gauze, followed by a bit of tape to hold the bandage in place. The doctor approached 62 and bent over to look him in the eye.

"Boy, isn't it true that you suffer from an anomaly?" The doctor didn't wait for a response. He lurched forward and added, "And wouldn't you like to be repaired?"

62 looked back at the frightening doctor without blinking. "No. I was mistaken. I do not require any assistance."

The Way Back 27

It was a long walk back to the pods from the doctor's room. At one point, 62 thought about how much easier the trip had been resting on the slim white bed with wheels. Then he changed his mind. It might be far, but he'd rather walk than get handled by Machines like that again.

"Are you doing okay?" 71 slowed his pace so that he could fall into the same tentative step as 62.

"I think so." 62 wasn't sure if he would ever be okay again, but didn't want to let 71 know that.

"I'm glad that I made it to you in time. The treatment they were administering is unpredictable." The teacher looked at his student with tender affection. "There's no telling what could have happened to you. I might never have seen you again."

62 stopped in the hallway a few paces from the elevator door. "The Keepers showed me pictures of other Boys who were treated with that thing." He shuddered. "I'm glad I didn't end up like them."

71 placed his hand on 62's shoulder and squeezed it gently. The old Man then took the last few steps toward the steel door and pressed the down arrow on the panel beside it. The red ring of light encircled the button, and the two figures began their wait for the door to open.

"We have to discuss the issue of your dreams. I should have taught you to shield them from others much sooner. I wasn't aware that the doctor had found a way to monitor them." 71 sighed with exhaustion. "He has always had such a linear mind; I didn't think that he would ever discover dreaming at all. I suppose even old Men can learn new tricks."

62 closed his eyes and fought the urge to throw up. All of this focus on his dreams had his stomach in knots. Just thinking about the doctor being in his mind, and the resulting treatment, made him ill.

"You told me that there were others who could see my dreams the way you do." 62 tried to keep calm, but an edge of anger rose in his voice. "Why didn't you tell me that dreams were so bad? That Man in there wants to put electricity in my brain because of it."

"I know." 71's reply was quiet and trembled slightly. "I'm terribly sorry that this happened. I'm going to help you protect yourself so Men like that won't be aware of your abilities. If you trust me, and follow my instruction, then you will be safe."

"But they already know I dream!" 62's shout echoed down the empty corridor. "They already know I see things when I sleep. The doctor has even been in my dream before. He knows I can talk to people in my dreams, too."

"Trust me, 62. This is not the first case of dreaming that I have taken care of." 71 tapped the down arrow again, but nothing seemed to happen in response to his impatient button pushing.

"Not the first?" A hot swell of anger filled his chest, causing his voice to crack. "There have been others? And where are they?"

71 grabbed hold of 62's flailing arms and held them down to the Boy's side. "No, not the first, and not the last either. Some of them have grown up to be Men with careers throughout Adaline. A few of them have gone on to supervise others in the Community and flourish in their positions. They use their imagination to help shape our world and influence the Community. But many of them become reckless and end up in places like this. Taken, and never seen or heard from again. Not in the classroom, and not in dreams. Dreamers can be stripped from their pods and stolen away from Adaline altogether.

"You must trust me, 62. You have got to listen to what I will teach you and put it into practice. Because if you don't, you'll be lost forever."

62 ceased his struggle against his teacher. His eyes filled with the blur of tears, and then suddenly he was crying. 71 released his grip on 62's arms and slid his hands up and around the Boy's back until the two figures were entwined in embrace. 62's sobs grew in intensity, but they were muffled by the old teacher's tunic and the protective cover of his thick, flowing beard.

"I d-don't want to be l-lost," 62 stuttered once he found a break in his sobs. "I just want t-to be a g-good Boy."

71 hugged 62 tight and whispered, "You are a good Boy. You are also very special to me, and to Adaline. I don't know when, but I promise your dreams and drawings will prove to be valuable in time. You will one day have the power to make Adaline better for all Men."

The heavy door leading to the elevator box slid open quietly. 62 pulled away from his teacher and wiped his eyes. 71 pressed his hand against the door, preventing it from closing before the pair made their way inside.

62 started to take a step toward the elevator, then stopped again and looked up at 71. Through still-wet eyes, the outline of the teacher was blurry. "What is grass?"

71 looked shocked at the question and took a moment to think before responding. He pieced together the connection between the question and the rough doctor

they'd just left and shook his head in disgust. "It is a common name for the Poa Pratensis you've seen in your dreams. 'Grass' is only used by those who are uneducated and unwilling to use the proper name for things."

62 nodded, satisfied with the answer. "I want to go back to my cube."

"So do I," 71 agreed. "We have just one stop to make before we go back." His slender finger pressed a button on the inside of the elevator and the tiny box began its quiet descent to level B15.

The Overwrite 28

The door opened to reveal a room larger than any 62 had ever seen before. It dwarfed the long corridors of his pod, and even made the Dressing Hall seem insignificant and cramped. Although the bright white ceiling wasn't particularly high, the walls were spaced far enough for all of C.A.T. to be dropped down inside them with room to spare.

71 stepped out of the elevator and took a few strides before realizing that 62 was not following. He turned and waved his hand at the young Boy.

"It's okay. Come on. We don't have much time before someone realizes you have taken a detour. We must act quickly."

62 stayed in the elevator and shook his head. The door started to slide shut. 71 leaped back and put his hand against the edge of the door just before it sealed closed. The door obediently opened again in response to his touch.

"I wish we had time to stand here and discuss this, but we do not. Come with me." 71 took 62's hand in his own and tugged until the Boy took a step forward.

"What is this place? I want to know what's happening." 62 pulled away and pressed himself against the back wall of the compartment.

"This is where one of my good brothers works. Somewhere forgotten by most of the Community. Please, 62, you must trust me. We are losing valuable time."

71 didn't wait for a response. He grasped 62's hand and pulled him out of the elevator. 71 took long, hurried strides into the vast emptiness of the room and 62 struggled to keep up. They walked a dozen paces into the space before 62 could see where they were heading.

He didn't like what he saw.

Far in the distance lay a thin white bed with slender steel legs. Several low tables surrounded the bed with a number of shiny instruments lined in rows atop them. Lights shone down on the lab, making the entire scene so white and shimmering that it blended into the distant walls in the background.

62 gasped, then twisted his wrist until it slipped through his teacher's grasp. Before he could process another thought, his feet took off with him and soon 62 found himself sprinting across the room toward a far corner.

The bright lights, empty space, and monochromatic landscape disoriented 62. He ran blindly toward one of the far walls in hopes that he would find a door or some other method of escape. The sound of his racing heart filled his ears and drowned out 71's shouts as he called after him.

62 reached the wall and began running his hands all over it, searching for a sensor or control panel. Finding nothing, he spun and moved to his right, running his hands frantically over the stark white panels. Suddenly, 71 was upon him and grabbed at his tunic. The fabric tore as 62 bolted again. The attempt to get away ended when 62 found himself in a corner with 71 right behind him.

"You're going to strap me down to a bed to repair me!" 62 spat with fury.

71 grasped 62 around the wrist with more determination than he had before. He panted from the sprint across the great room. He was not angry so much as tired and out of breath.

"No, Brother. It's not the same. I promise." 71 moved back toward the bed and tables. He marched across the room with resolve, dragging 62 behind him.

"It looks the same!" 62 tried to pull away but his teacher's grip would not break.

"Trust me." 71 didn't explain further.

62 fought 71's tight grip the entire way to where the bed and tables stood. He shouted randomly at the empty room and cried tears of rage. He thrashed about wildly and his eyes were so swollen with tears that he didn't notice the Man seated amongst the equipment.

"Brother!" The Man stood up and reached out to embrace 71. The motion was stopped midair when he noticed 62. "You never do just stop by to say hello, do you? Always a problem or project to work on."

71 nodded and pointed with his off-hand to 62 who was still pulling against his grip with all his might. "We need some help, and I'm afraid we don't have much time. This isn't exactly a scheduled visit for our young brother, here."

"I see, I see. Well, what exactly is the matter, then?" The Man kneeled down and peered at 62's writhing figure.

"He needs help from a doctor who knows what he's doing."

"No, I don't!" 62 shrieked and pulled hard on 71's hand. He could feel his wrist slipping. He changed directions and pulled again; the grip broke and 62 was suddenly free. He misjudged his footing and landed hard on the floor. The wind was knocked from his chest and in the moment that it took him to get back to his feet, the new doctor had grabbed hold of his ankle.

"Our young friend here has been to see a doctor once already, I take it?" The doctor pushed the tails of his white lab coat back behind him and picked 62 up. He carried 62 toward the bed, being careful to make sure he avoided contact with the kicks and punches that assailed him. His beard was much shorter than 71's, and he lifted his chin in an attempt to keep the closely groomed bristles out of 62's grasp.

"Yes, we just came from level 2." 71 helped the doctor get 62 to sit up on the bed. Once the Boy was in place, 71 bent down to hold his feet to keep them from kicking any of the nearby instruments.

"Level 2?" The Man looked with great concern at 62. "Not many come back from there." 71's doctor turned his face toward 62. "I'm sorry that you had to endure whatever trials led you there, little one. I am very sincere when I tell you that I am glad to see you made it out intact, and if I were you, I'd never want to see another doctor again either."

The sad expression and quiet sympathy caught 62's attention and he stopped flailing. He looked at the new doctor, and then at 71. Both Men looked worried. The moment he stopped struggling both Men let go of his limbs.

"Do you put electricity in brains?" 62 looked around at the tables and didn't see any boxes with dials and wires.

"No, I certainly do not. I've seen it done once, when I was in the introductory Defensive Medical program. Lucky for me, I didn't have the stomach for it, so they assigned me to Biomedical Connectivity Repair. Much less screaming and fewer broken bones involved." The doctor moved around as he spoke and began picking up a few small items, placing them on a hover tray that followed close behind him.

"What is Biomumical Connoductor Repair?" 62 followed the doctor with his eyes and paid close attention to each tool on the tray.

"Biomedical Connectivity Repair," 71 corrected. "When you are animated, a sensor is deposited into the lining of your stomach. Then, a tiny microchip is implanted under the skin in your neck to record and transmit your vital biological data to the sensors in your cube. Whenever there is a break in that communication, either because of damage or malfunction, the affected are brought here to have the break repaired."

The doctor added in, "Although admittedly, I don't see many patients. The ingestible event markers and radio frequency identification chips are practically indestructible. It leaves me with a lot of time on my hands."

71 chuckled, as the doctor winked at him. His tray full, the doctor pulled a hover chair over to the bed and sat down. The tray, now holding several small devices, came to a rest at the head of the bed.

"So, who are you?" 62 asked while he ogled the items on the tray. There was a small box that looked like a scanner, a small shiny tool with a very sharp tip, a band of twisted wire with two small panes of glass inserted into it, and a container with dozens of tiny black Machines that almost resembled the Tapinoma Sessile from his dream.

"Oh, silly me. Always missing introductions. I am 2442, and I bid thee welcome to my lab." The doctor lowered his chin to his chest and extended his right arm out toward 62.

"The doctor with a flair for the dramatic." 71 rolled his eyes.

"True, true." 42 agreed and then winked. "But I'm also the doctor with the cure for what ails you."

42 picked up the wire with glass and put the contraption on his face. The ends of the wire wrapped around his ears and the two glass panes rested perfectly in front of 42's eyes. When the doctor noticed 62's curious stare he said, "Optical magnification glasses. They help me to see things that are very small."

The Man peered over the lenses to look at the tray, then picked up the scanner and turned it on. It beeped and chirped in response. The doctor put the scanner against 62's neck. He waved it slowly back and forth over the back of the neck, hovering just above the skin. The box chirped again.

"Ah, there you are." 42 grinned. He reached toward the tray and picked up the thin steel instrument. "This will hurt a bit but try not to flinch."

A sharp pain pricked the back of 62's neck as the doctor cut into his flesh. He couldn't help but pull away from the sharp knife. "Ow! That hurts! What are you doing?"

"Stay still please," 42 commanded. "I am removing the chip under your skin. This will only take a moment. The doctor pressed the knife in again, moved it slightly and then pulled it away from 62's neck. "Got it. Now, for your replacement."

42 picked up one of the tiny black devices from the tray and put it into a tube attached to a long needle. "This will also sting a bit."

62 couldn't see the needle press into the flesh of his neck, but he certainly could feel the tip break through. "Ouch!"

"There, all done." 42 placed his tools back on the tray and put something wet over the cut and puncture point on the back of 62's neck. "This is some antiseptic to keep your injuries from being infected. It will also seal that cut up for you. With any luck it will heal and remain unnoticed by the Keepers."

"So he will now be undetected?" 71 leaned behind the bed to get a better look at 62's new injuries.

"Yes. The subdermal implant will now be transmitting benign data from one of the most average and uneventful Men to ever have walked the halls of Adaline. No matter how excited or upset our little friend gets, his vitals will always report as normal. There will never again be any report received by the Community of an elevated heart rate or imbalance of hormones."

71 lifted his eyebrows with curiosity. "Whose data will they be reading, exactly?"

42 chuckled, "Why the good doctor on level 2, of course."

X-CURSE

The Private Tutoring

29

62 entered the pod, escorted by a single Transportation Aide. His reemergence into C.A.T. was much less dramatic than his exit had been. All of the other Boys were still tucked away and asleep in their cubes. Their unified breathing and the rare rustle of blankets on steel was all that could be heard in the pod.

The door to 62's cube slid open, and the Transportation Aide waited for him to get in and pull out his blanket before it locked the door behind him. 62 was so tired that he didn't bother to check his chute for dinner. The moment he was comfortable, sleep came to him and consumed him in the darkness.

"Welcome back," 71's voice echoed from somewhere inside 62's mind. "It's good to see you again."

A tiny light shone in the distance, and 62 floated toward it. His dream was dark aside from the pinhole light, but he wasn't afraid. His limbs all drifted easily through the dark and he enjoyed the relaxing sensation of flying.

"Where are you?" 62 tried to reach the light, but it seemed to never get any closer. "What is this place?"

"I'm in my own dream. What do you see in yours?" 71's voice was whispery and small as if he were speaking through a crack in a wall.

"Just darkness with a little light. I think it's moving." 62 stopped trying to reach the tiny glow. Once he stopped moving, it seemed to float back toward him.

"The light is the connection between us. I've spent some time the last few cycles working on ways to teach you to block your consciousness from outside viewing."

The glowing light was almost within 62's reach now, and he extended his hand to try and grasp it. When his fingers touched the warm smoldering connection, it zipped backward out of his reach and hung in the air over him.

"Why can't I see anything?" 62 spoke toward the light.

"Most of the structure of the dreams we've shared has been constructed by my consciousness. Even when you were dreaming on your own, our connection fed your dreams. Now that I'm blocking my consciousness from yours, it will be up to you to reconstruct your landscapes using your own creativity."

The glowing light started to burn intensely and changed color from white to blue. A small red flame emerged from the blue light, and it sparked and crackled against the dark backdrop. The ball of fire grew until it was the size of a tablet, then the size of a hover table, and finally the size of a Man. A hand emerged from the center of the flame.

62 drifted backward in the darkness, startled by the wriggling hand grasping at the air in his dream. A long cable dropped down from somewhere high above the flame and the hand grabbed hold. It tugged the line, causing it to go rigid. A second hand appeared and grasped the cable above the first. 62 watched as the pair of hands struggled on the cable. A moment later, an entire body emerged from the

flames and the light burnt out, leaving 62 completely immersed in the dark.

"I really hate going through all this. It's so much easier to share dreams with someone whose consciousness is open." 71 spoke as if he were directly in front of 62. "Oh, my. It really is dark in here, isn't it?"

"There was a light, but it just burnt out." 62 reached his hands out in front of him and felt the edge of 71's tunic.

"Well, whose fault is that?" The teacher's hand grasped 62's. "I can't share my dream ability with you now. It's all up to you. Go ahead, put something out there, will you?"

62 closed his eyes and tried to imagine what it would look like if they were standing in the wide spaces of previous dreams. He opened his eyes and found that he and 71 were standing on a small patch of terra a couple of meters wide. Out in the distance, groups of blue, green and brown were splattered across the landscape. Enough light shone out from the blue patches to illuminate the Boy and his Teacher. 62 looked up at 71 and shrugged his shoulders.

"Well, decent enough for now. I won't be here long, so it will do." 71 sat down on the brown patch and crossed his legs beneath him. He looked up into 62's face and smiled.

62 copied his teacher and the two sat in silence for a moment. All of the patches in color shifted, growing and shrinking in turn as 62 tried to keep their images stable in his dream while thinking back on the events of the past few cycles. Flashes of the doctor's laboratories, long passageways, and elevator doors passed over a few of the patches nearby.

"It is a lot to take in." 71 said quietly. He wrapped his arm over 62's shoulders. "You've done very well with all of the challenges that have come your way. I am very proud of all that you have accomplished."

62 shrugged and the images vanished from the pools of blue light. "So what now? If you closed my dreams off, does that mean I can't see yours anymore?"

"For the moment, yes. In time, you will be stronger, and we will be able to reopen the connection between us. But first I need to teach you how to protect your consciousness from viewing. It's going to take some practice, but I know you are strong enough to do it."

62 nodded although he didn't quite understand. "So no one else can see my dreams now either?"

"No one. Not even me, unless you allow me to. If someone tries, there will be a small light just like the one that I came through. When you see a light, if you don't recognize the voice speaking to you all you have to do is wake yourself up and they won't be able to come through."

"What if I can't wake up?"

"If you ever feel like you can't wake up, then there is a real problem. Hold your breath until you can feel your lungs burning. Eventually, the oxygen deprivation will cause your brain to force your body awake so that you can breathe again. It's a natural response to prevent suffocation during sleep."

62 held his breath until his lungs began to burn and all of the images around them began to fade. Before they faded completely, he exhaled and resumed his breathing, and the images became bright and vivid again. He looked up at 71. "How do you know all of this stuff?"

71 grinned, "When I was a Boy, I paid very close attention to my studies."

The Dodge 30

All eyes were on 62 as he entered the classroom and sat down at his desk. He tried not to notice, but his skin prickled, and his heart pounded from the attention. He forced his gaze up from the floor and focused on 99. 62 lifted his lips in an attempt at a smile and shrugged his shoulders.

"Where were you last cycle?" One of the Boys seated near the door shouted over the din of whispers that filled the class.

62 turned in the direction of the questioning voice but didn't focus on any one Boy in particular. Instead, he stared at the wall above their heads, too uncomfortable to look his brothers in the face.

"I had to go someplace." 62 wasn't sure how to answer the question. Even he wasn't quite sure where he had been, or how he could explain what had happened to him. There was certainly no good way to describe the elevator or the other floors in Adaline.

"I heard you got the fog," someone seated to his right piped in.

62 looked down at the empty floor in the middle of the classroom and shook his head. "Nope, no fog."

"Were you bad?" 99's question was the first that was filled with audible concern.

"I don't think so. No, I wasn't bad. I didn't get in trouble or anything. I just had to go away for a while."

"Are you unwell?" When a Boy to his left asked the question, everyone instinctively scooted a few inches away from 62.

"No. Well, I don't think so." 62 looked up at the sound of the door.

71 strolled in, a smile on his face and a spring in his step. 62 again felt rescued by his teacher's entrance. The uncomfortable squirming in his stomach lessened when most of the other Boys in the room turned their attention to the Man.

71 busied himself at his desk for a moment then casually looked around the classroom. When he saw 62 seated in his usual spot, the teacher gasped loudly.

"Well, well! Who do we have here?" The teacher waved his arms too much and his voice took on a strange pitch as he made a poor attempt at acting surprised. "Brother 62, back from his adventures! Welcome back, young student. We have missed you these few cycles and are so pleased to be blessed with your acquaintance once more."

"Uh, glad to be back...I guess." 62's cheeks flushed in embarrassment.

"Our young brother here," 71's arms made a great arc in the air before finally pointing at 62, "was chosen for some special training over the past few cycles. Unfortunately, he is not at liberty to share many details with the class, so please don't pester him with too many questions." 71's strained voice cracked as he spoke and his feet fidgeted across the floor as he tried to appear... well, no one could figure out how 71 was trying to appear.

Suspicious eyebrows lifted across the room. All of the Boys began looking back and forth between the awkward teacher and the deflated student. While 71 was exuberantly putting on a show, 62 was doing his best to curl up into a tiny little ball and disappear.

Several hands rose throughout the group. 71 shuffled several awkward steps toward the center of the room, his hips swaying and knees locking in an odd march that looked completely unnatural. He bent suddenly at the waist and pointed at a Boy whose hand was raised. "Yes? Your question please."

"Why are you talking like that?"

71 straightened until he was as straight and rigid as a steel wall. He pushed his shoulders out wide, placed his hands on his hips and thrust his pelvis forward. His head snapped to the left so that he gazed over his shoulder and in a booming voice he replied, "Talking like what, exactly?"

"Like that." Confusion filled the Boy's voice.

"Yeah. And why are you moving around like that?" Another Boy from across the room chimed in. "Are you unwell?"

71 dragged his feet in a circle as he turned around. His hands fanned out and his fingers wiggled wildly at his sides. "Whatever do you mean? This is how I always talk and move. It's completely natural."

62 slouched farther in his chair. Although now all eyes were on the teacher, for some reason he felt even more embarrassed than before. He closed his eyes and rested his head on the desk, hoping 71's antics would end.

"Uh, actually," 99 snickered, "you kind of look like a Keeper who's had one too many turns at the charging station."

The entire class broke out in giggles. 71's eyes widened, and he approached 62's desk in a gait that exaggerated his already flamboyant body movements.

"Why, I do declare that I don't know whatsoever you might mean." 71 bent again and touched 62's desk with the edge of his fingertips. "62 has just returned from parts unknown, and I am pleased to meet his acquaintance once again."

Everyone looked at 62.

"You're like this because of him?" 99 pointed at 62 with accusation. "Yup, I was right. He's unwell. Must be a virus that can be shared, too. Look at what it did to the teacher."

73 nodded. "We should do something about it. I don't want to end up like that."

"Let's call a Keeper or something. Get these two virus holders out of here." 85 got up from his desk and started toward the panel on the wall beside the door.

The teacher snapped out of his dramatic act. "You will do no such thing. Sit down! No one here has a virus. Holy dustblowers! What is wrong with you Boys?" He shook his head and moved back toward the front of the room in his normal gait with arms tucked naturally beneath his beard.

"So, you're okay?"

As 12 posed the question each of the students in the front of the classroom pushed their desks away from the teacher's desk.

"Yes, I'm perfectly fine. Average by all accounts." 71 tapped at his tablet and the day's lesson, a diagram titled "Damaged Keeper Neurosystems", appeared on the wall behind him.

"And he's…he's okay too?" 56 pointed at 62.

"Yes, yes. He's average as well. Just back from doing whatever he was doing." 71 waved his hand in 62's general direction with annoyance. "Let's forget about welcoming him back into the group and just move on with today's lesson. This diagram shows the neural pathways that augment the scope of vision in Keepers and other Machines like them. As you can see, the visual input connections are located in quadrant A…"

62 shrunk down beneath his desk and stared at his feet while the rest of the Boys stared at the projected lesson in confusion. No one followed what was taught that day.

Instead, the group of Boys just looked around in puzzlement until the tones rang.

155

The awkwardness of 62's return to class faded into the normal repetition of C.A.T. The only brother who still seemed to have any concern was 99, who arrived in the Dressing Hall every morning ready to see how 62 was doing, and to assault him with questions about where he had been.

"Hello. Sleep well?" 99 examined 62's face with intense scrutiny.

"Fine, again. How are you?" 62 rolled his eyes and tried to flatten the knots in his hair from his rough night of sleep.

"Oh, you know, the usual." 99 sniffed 62's tunic and scrunched his nose at some imagined smell.

"Stop doing that!" 62 stepped as far ahead of 99 in the line as he could, doing his best to not bump into the Boy in front of him. 99 simply followed along.

"Doing what?" 99 bent down to look at 62's hands.

62 pulled his hands up into the sleeves of his tunic and tucked them under his armpits. "Stop doing…whatever you're doing. I've told you a thousand times. I'm fine. Nothing happened. Like the teacher said I just went to some training thing and now I'm back."

"Mmm hmmm." 99 nodded, then plucked a piece of lint off of 62's sleeve and eyed it carefully. "I know the story. I just don't believe it. When are you going to tell me what happened?"

Although 62 was irritated with the constant stream of questions from 99, he also burned with the desire to share his experiences. Out of all the Boys in C.A.T., 99 was his closest brother. After all that had happened though, 62 wasn't sure that he could trust 99 with so many secrets.

"I've told you what I can. I can't tell you anymore. I'm sworn to secrecy." 62 raised his chin a little in mock importance.

"Swore your secrecy to who?" 99 took a step forward as the line progressed. "Did you have to swear secrecy to the Machines? Did they program you?"

"Program me? What are you talking about?" 62 did his best to not raise his voice even though he was aggravated.

"One of the cycles when you were gone, we learned about how you can program a Machine to behave or react a certain way. It all has to do with the boards and circuits. Did they circuit you?" 99 started pulling at 62's hair, parting it and looking for an access panel.

62 pulled away and turned slightly to try and keep 99 from noticing the tiny scar left over from his chip removal. He batted 99's hands away from his head. "You're talking a bunch of nonsense. Knock it off. You're going to get us into trouble."

"Well, there wouldn't be any trouble if you'd just tell me what's going on with you." 99 pouted, injured by 62's refusal to tell him about his experiences.

"Fine. Yes, I've been reprogrammed." 62 made his legs go rigid and stuck his hands out straight in front of him.

He took two awkward steps forward as the line moved and pretended to be a Machine. "Beep-beep-boop. I-am-a-Boy. Beep-boop-beep. I-have-come-to-infiltrate-you. Boop-boop-beep. Take-me-to-your-showers."

99 laughed. "So it is true. You are a Machine."

62 cocked his head mechanically and made a hissing sound as he turned to look at 99. "What-do-you-mean. I-am-producing-conversation-at-optimal-levels." 62 pretended to have a hiccup in his programming. "I-I-I-I." He shook his head abruptly from left to right. "I-am-like-every-other-Boy."

99's chuckles erupted into hysterics and Boys from the surrounding lines began to turn and look. Soon several Boys were pointing and laughing at 62's antics. He smiled at them all, returned to his normal self and waved at the crowd.

Two Keepers who had noticed the laughter began to make their way toward the group and all of the Boys returned their attention to the lines ahead of them. 62 and 99 faced forward as well, although instead of dropping his hands to his sides and frowning in boredom like everyone else, 99 used his palms to wipe the tears of laughter from his eyes.

The Keepers determined that the disturbance had ended and confirmed that all of the Boys were in their place. And, after looking through the lines with flashing blue eyes, they returned to their posts.

Once the Machines were out of earshot 99 continued to peck at 62. "Well, I don't know what's been happening to you. But something about you is different."

"What's that supposed to mean?" 62 turned just enough to see 99 out of the corner of his eye. "I'm just the same as you, and everybody else around here. Bored and wishing I knew what the heck we're learning all this junk for."

99 shook his head. "No, you're not. I don't know what it is, but you change a little more every day. It's almost like you know something. Something that no one else knows."

"I know a bit less than the rest of you. Between the fog and my trip to the doctor, I've missed a fair amount of class." 62 took a step forward. He hadn't realized that it was his turn for the shower and was surprised when he was pulled forward into the receptacle by an Aide.

"What's a doctor?" 99 shouted from behind him.

62 was stripped of his clothes and he covered his eyes with his hands as cleaning fluid fell down over his body.

He had said too much.

62 closed his eyes and fell into sleep. He imagined the classroom, the one place he knew better than anywhere else. Although his focus still wasn't as strong as it had been with 71's help, he was able to form the walls, floor, and a single desk and hover chair. He sat down in the chair and pushed it back and forth across the floor from one end of the room to the other.

A pinhole of light, barely noticeable, gleamed down from the vast empty black above the room. 62 heard the whisper of a voice creeping through.

"62, I'm coming in." 71's voice cracked and echoed from far away.

"Passcode?" 62 asked calmly.

The glimmer of light dimmed as 71 stopped pushing through. The whisper repeated, "Passcode?"

"Yeah. Our tablets are passcode protected. I figured I should have one, too." 62 tapped his feet on the floor.

"That's a great idea, but I don't know what it is yet." 71's whisper crackled and then the light shone bright again as he pushed through the block on 62's consciousness. There was a large crackle and then 71 appeared in the classroom.

"I think the passcode should be something that you and I know, but no one else could." 62 put his hand on the desk and closed his eyes, trying to imagine the book that 71 had shown him before. There was a small puff of smoke that emerged, but nothing else. "I can't make that book appear. Can you do it?"

"My abilities to create things are greatly minimized because of the block on your dreams. But you can lend me some of your power and then I might be able to manage something. We should use a text that is more obscure than the one I showed you though; something that only those dreamers who have our best interests in mind would have access to."

"There are more books?" 62 asked as 71 pressed a firm hand on his shoulder. Immediately, 62 could feel his energy draining through his shoulder and entering the warm center of 71's palm. His vision dimmed as energy trickled out of his body.

"Oh, yes. There are many books. Most of them about Adaline's humble beginnings and the Community's instructions on keeping order. But there are a few that our Father kept purely for entertainment." 71 closed his eyes and placed his other hand palm-up in front of him. His palm glowed and a frame the size of a book formed in the air. A cover materialized and then stacks of pages filled the gap from front to back. Once complete, the book fell from the air into 71's outstretched hand.

62 gasped and heaved. Sweat dripped from his brow and his hands shook. The draw of energy made him exhausted, and the area in his shoulder where it had escaped into 71 burned and ached. He doubled over with tears in his eyes and panted, trying to stop the spinning of his mind.

As 62 regained his composure, the dim light surrounding the two figures regained its vibrancy. 71 kneeled down in front of the Boy and placed the book on the desk.

"I hope you're alright. I had forgotten what a task it can be for a beginner to share energy with someone. Luckily, the book is here, and I think I know just the word to use for your passcode."

The black spine of the book was emblazoned with gold text that read, "H.G. Wells" and the front had an image of a dilapidated building printed on it. A white space on the cover held words that proclaimed, "War of the Worlds". 71 opened the book gingerly and began slowly turning the pages.

"What does that mean?" 62 craned his head to look at the open cover of the book held in his teacher's hands.

71 replied casually. "Oh, war is the idea that when two separate groups aren't getting along, they will automatically resort to physical altercation. It's an archaic theory that the Defense group is always preparing for, although it's never happened. For one thing, there have never been two separate groups in all of Adaline history. It's just us Men and our Machines."

"What's a world?" 62 stood up a little from his chair and tried to decipher the upside-down words written on the pages as 71 slowly read through them.

"Well, Adaline is the world." 71 snorted in laughter then added, "This book entertains a theory that there could be more than one world. It's a ridiculous notion but makes for some entertaining reading. Ah, here. 'Chobham' would make a wonderful passcode. I doubt there is a Man in all of Adaline who could guess it, even if he were trying."

"What's a Chobham?" 62 tried to read the passage above 71's finger but couldn't quite make out the words.

"It's the name of a place where beings from another world land before their attack. The Men there don't realize the danger and get vaporized." 71 snapped the pages shut and turned the book over in his hands until it disappeared.

"Chobham." 62 repeated again. "What if I can't remember it?"

71 smiled. "It's simple, Brother. Just don't forget."

The Inner Mind

33

99 came barreling down the hall outside of the classroom, pushing Boys out of his way and shouting each time his path was blocked. 62 had successfully avoided him for several cycles. 62 was too afraid of letting any more secrets slip out accidentally. Avoiding his brother hadn't been easy though, and his evasion tactics had finally failed.

"There you are! I've been trying to talk to you forever. But you've been late to class, first to leave. And have you been skipping showers or something? I haven't seen you in the Dressing Hall, either."

"You can't skip showers. You have to take one to get fresh clothes and get to class." 62's crass response seemed to go unnoticed.

"It's like you're hiding out in your cube or something. Which doesn't make any sense because it's boring in there." 99's eyebrow raised in curiosity. "Isn't it? Or have you changed your feelings about that?"

“Of course it’s boring in the cubes. There’s nothing to do in there but swallow pills and sleep.” 62 stifled a grin as he thought briefly about his dreams and how well they had been progressing within the safety of his newly blocked consciousness.

99 noticed the edges of the smirk on 62. “Right. I still don’t get it. What’s going on with you?”

“Nothing worth talking about.” 62 took the last few steps into the classroom and headed toward his desk at the back of the room. 99 followed and sat down beside him.

“So then, what was that you said about a doctor?” 99 spoke quietly enough that the other Boys in the room didn’t seem to overhear.

62 waited a moment just in case, and once it was clear none of the other Boys were paying attention he whispered, “I’m not supposed to talk about that. It’s just like 71 told the class. I went for some training, and it took a couple of cycles to get through. When it was done and I had a chance to get better, they let me come back to class.”

99’s eyebrows went even farther up his forehead. “Get better? Was something wrong with you? Some of the others said you caught a virus. Is that true?”

62 smacked his forehead with his hand. “No, I didn’t catch a virus. I don’t even think Boys can get viruses.”

“So what’s a doctor then?” When it was apparent that 62 wasn’t going to do any more than continue to shake his head, 99 pleaded. “Come on. I’m your best brother. I promise not to tell anyone else. You can tell me about whatever is going on with you.”

62 groaned. “Fine. The doctor is a Man who tries to fix anomalies that happen in Boys. So, if a Boy like me is doing something that he isn’t supposed to, the doctor tries to fix him. “

“You were doing something bad?” 99 was shocked. “Did you try to escape like 00?"

“No, nothing like that.” 62 tried to figure out if there was a way to explain his dreaming in a way that 99 could understand. "I was just… thinking about things I shouldn't have been."

99 scrunched his face, further confused by the explanation. "How could anyone know what you were thinking? That doesn't make any sense."

"I know it doesn't. But that's how it is. Sometimes they can see your thoughts. And if you aren't thinking what you're supposed to think, they send you for lessons with the doctor who tries to make you think right again." The more 62 talked about the experience, the more he hoped no one could hear the conversation.

"So you're thinking right again?" 99 looked sorrowfully into 62's eyes.

"Yeah, sure. Right enough, anyway." 62 grinned as convincingly as he could.

The tones in the hallway sung their song and the teacher entered the room just before the door slid closed. He did his usual short preparation at the head of the class and put a diagram up on the wall. "Are there any questions about the last few classes before we dive back into Neurosystems?"

99 raised his hand and 62 dropped his head to his desk in desperation.

"Yes, 99?" 71 looked at the Boy and then to 62, who was now covering his head with his arms and moaning.

"Why do Machines use Neurosystems?"

62 peeked up at his brother from beneath the crease of his arms, surprised that 99 hadn't asked the teacher more about doctors and thought viewing.

"It's quite simple, really. The Machines' viewing platform is made up of cameras and screens that would normally only display in two dimensions. It's similar to looking at something on your tablet, or viewing a lesson projected on the wall. It's flat and has no depth. For example, in this diagram that we will be studying today, it's impossible to know if wires A, F and J are affixed above or below B, D and Y unless you are referencing a key or set of instructions that lists their position in relationship to one another.

"So for the Machines to 'see', they have been fitted with a Neurosystems network that creates a three-dimensional plane in their central processing unit. This allows them to recognize each of us in our full depth. It helps them to see that our ears are located behind our eyes. It helps them to understand how long a tunnel is and helps to identify that when we are standing in line, we are not a single Man standing in front of them, but that we are hundreds of Men in a line stacked one behind the other."

99 nodded, jotted a note down on his tablet to save for later and thanked the teacher for the explanation. He casually glanced at 62's stunned face and shrugged. "What?"

62 shook his head, turned on his tablet and did his best to listen to the lesson.

"Chobham."

It was amazing that 62 was able to hear the whisper over the pile of grinding gears that writhed and ticked against one another in his dream. He had been trying to dream up a Keeper so he could practice giving the Machines directions.

The small voice passed by his ear like a heavy breath, and he turned to see if someone was standing behind him. Instead, he found a small tear in the wall with the familiar glowing light shining through. He moved away from the table and looked at the light closely. Within the glowing ball of light he could see the faint outline of a head with its ear pressed against the other side of the rift.

"Come in." 62 spoke the welcome directly into the light and then took a step back so there would be room for the Man's body to pass through. 71 pressed his body through the thin crack and 62 marveled at how the teacher was able to warp and melt his body to make it thin enough to pass through the small opening.

"I've brought a friend." 71 pushed his arm back through the still glimmering light up to his shoulder and winced as he tried to grasp something on the other side. He added through clenched teeth, "I hope you don't mind."

62 shook his head and stared intently at the hole that was stuffed full of 71's wriggling shoulder. The Man found whatever he had been blindly searching for and pulled back hard. The teacher struggled against the narrow opening and pressed both feet against the dream-wall to use as leverage against the weight of what he was trying to pull through. 62 got behind his teacher, grasped him around the waist and helped pull with all of his might. Finally the teacher's arm inched out of the crevice. His elbow emerged, then his wrist, and finally his hand which clasped an identical hand.

The stranger's wrist appeared, and then his elbow, and inch by inch the rest of his body pulled through the tiny opening. Once the Man's head emerged, both shoulders shot through the tight gap with a loud "Pop!" The rest of his body was quick to follow. The three bodies tumbled into 62's dream, landing in a tangle of limbs.

Luckily for the three of them, falling in dreams caused no damage to their bodies and they simply untangled themselves from one another and wiped the dust from their tunics.

Once he righted himself, 62 was surprised to recognize Doctor 2442 from level B15. His finely groomed white beard danced on his jowls as he twisted his face to and fro. The doctor tapped the side of his head with the heel of his hand and winced.

"I NEVER DO GET USED TO GETTING AROUND LIKE THAT." The doctor shouted toward 71. "MAKES MY EARS GET ALL PLUGGED UP."

71 shook his head and smiled. He walked behind his brother and rubbed behind the doctor's earlobes with his fingers in gentle circles. "There, is that better?"

"What do you know, they popped! I still learn new things every day. Thank you. I'll have to remember that trick." Doctor 42 wiggled his jaw a little more and smiled at whatever sensation the movement gave him.

62 was puzzled. "I didn't know you could bring someone into my dream."

71 jumped in surprise at the sound of 62's voice as if he had forgotten where he was. "What's that? Oh, yes. You can travel with a companion. Or a hundred companions, if you like. It's all just a matter of having enough imagination."

71 and 42 noticed the writhing gears and wires clanging and tangling with one another on the table in the center of the room.

"What sort of experiment are we conducting?" 42 asked with excitement as he examined the chaos.

"It looks as if he's been trying to build something. But what kind of 'thing' is it? Very curious." 71 poked at a sprocket that bounced sporadically.

"Perhaps a miniature feeding apparatus?" The doctor pulled at a wire and tried to follow it through the mess to find its beginning and ending connections.

"Or maybe a transportation device. Note the wheels." The teacher ran his hand over a small wheel that rolled backward and forward all on its own.

"One of those Mobiles from Automata?" 42 touched 71's arm and closed his eyes. A thick book popped into the air in front of him and plopped open onto the table. 42 didn't delay in sifting through pages filled with black and white pictures.

"Oh, yes. Certainly a Mobile from Automata. But where is the steering harness?" 71 hunched over the textbook with his brother and the two mumbled together as they compared the pile of parts on the table with diagrams from the book.

"It's a Keeper." 62 approached the opposite end of the table. "Or at least, it was supposed to be."

"Oh." 42 said, eyeing the Boy.

"Dear." 71 added, looking up from the book at the flailing machine.

"I wanted to make one appear so that I could practice telling it what to do." A gear spun loose from its axle and flew up into the air, landing square in the center of 62's forehead.

"I see." Both Men spoke and stood in unison. The book vanished with a puff of smoke.

62 began to think he was doing something wrong and stumbled around trying to get the spinning gears, whirring sprockets, and rotating wheels to stop. "Not that I want the Keepers to do anything for me. I mean, nothing bad or anything. I just sometimes want them to do what I say."

71 crossed his arms, tucking them under his beard. 62 gently placed both of his hands in the deep pockets of his lab coat. Both nodded, a look of suspicion knitting between their bushy brows.

"Not that I'd make them do something they weren't supposed to. Or make them let me do something *I'm* not supposed to." The more flustered that 62 got, the less he was able to focus on the movements of the Machine in his dream. The heap began to wriggle and wrangle against itself until the entire mass was bouncing up and down on the table.

The two Men stepped back from the table to avoid being knocked over by a string of wires and clamps that might have been a mechanical fist. Neither spoke, and the firm set of their jaws did not change.

62 felt like he was digging himself into deeper trouble with his explanation, but he wasn't able to stop babbling on. "It's like when they're there and you want them to not be there and so you tell them and then they aren't there, but they're supposed to be there."

The bundle began to hiss and wheeze, steam pouring out of some unseen port. A head formed in the center of the fluctuating structure and let out a deep and haunting moan. The light above the room dimmed. The walls began to glow red-hot.

62 cried as the Machine, forming on its own in his dream, pulled itself together and got up from the table. It stood so high that its spiked head and glowing red eyes reached beyond the tops of the walls. Long jagged fingers pointed accusingly, and the giant Machine hissed, "1124562, you have been a very bad Boy."

62 turned to run from the mechanical creature but the walls pressed in on him. Tears streamed down his face, and he screamed in horror when he found himself trapped in a corner. The Keeper grabbed at his tunic and 62 could feel its molten hot fingers burning holes through the thin fabric.

"Enough!" 71 stepped forward and placed his hand on the left side of the writhing specter.

"Quite enough, indeed." The doctor moved to the other side of the Machine and placed his hand on it with a smack.

Both Men closed their eyes in unison and raised their off-hand out in front of them. They snapped their fingers, making a noise so soft that it couldn't be heard over the crashing noises of the rogue Machine. Instantly, the wretched thing vanished. The color of the room lifted, the temperature dropped, and silence filled the room.

62 collapsed to the floor. A few moments passed before he found the strength to wipe the tears from his eyes. "Th-thanks."

"Not a problem at all. Just remember, you've got to keep control of these dreams when you're in them. You never know what direction they will take if you let your imagination run away with them." 42 brushed his hand over a line of soot on his jacket left behind by the Machine and it vanished, returning the fabric to its bright white color.

"Very true, indeed." 71 knelt down in front of 62. "Exactly what is it that you want the Keepers to do for you?"

"I want them to leave me alone." 62 did his best not to whimper, but a small squeak escaped.

"I see." 71 looked into his young brother's eyes. "I don't think that's possible. The Keepers are there to take care of us, and to make sure that we are always well. That means they are always around. It's the only way for them to ensure we are good Boys and Men."

"I've done it before." 62 gasped once the words were out and he saw the look of astonishment on the two Men's faces.

"Really." The doctor sat down on the floor beside the teacher and his student. "Well, that does complicate things a bit then, doesn't it?"

"It might, indeed. Well, this brings us to why I've brought the good doctor to you tonight." 71 looked at both of his brothers with concern. "Do you remember the doctor you saw on Level 2?"

62 nodded and whispered, "Yes."

"Well, it seems that he remembers you, too."

62 awoke to find the doctor from level 2 standing outside the door to his cube. The Man's gaze was cast downward and 62 knew that he was reading the data stream displayed on the chest of the Keeper standing to his right. 62 closed his eyes tight and pretended to still be asleep.

"No more anomalies?" The doctor scratched his head. His brow wrinkled in frustration.

"No, Doctor. No further anomalies have been reported in connection with Boy 1124562. All vitals appear normal, and sleep cycles have improved into average range." The Keeper's eyes flashed blue as it relayed the data.

The terrifying doctor looked away from the Keeper at the cube across the hall. "Have symptoms spread to the surrounding Boys?"

"Negative. No further disruption has occurred within this section.

"Within this section?" The doctor jerked his head around to look back at the Keeper. "What about other sections of the pod? Have there been any anomalies reported?"

"Yes." The Keeper nodded its head with smooth hydraulic precision. "Another case was reported with Boy 1124999. The subject was animated in the same batch as Boy 1124562. I see they are also being trained in the same class, led by Man 2871."

The doctor peered into 62's cube and stared for a long time. It was all that 62 could do to keep his eyes from springing open when the Keeper mentioned his brother. The Man and Boy held a silent battle of wills, each waiting to see if 62 would flutter an eyelid and betray his thoughts.

After what seemed like an eternity, the sound of breakfast rolling down the tubes began prattling overhead. The doctor looked around, and realizing that the Boys were beginning to stir, marched quickly away. 62 sprung up from his place on the floor and pressed his face against the grating just in time to see the doctor heading in the direction of the Dressing Hall.

62 knew he'd have to act fast. He shoved his blanket into its chute. The instant his morning pills dropped through the tiny door above him, he extended his hand. Catching his breakfast in midair, he snapped the pills into his mouth and gulped them down without taking a drink.

A Keeper approached and began downloading his data. As they did every morning, its eyes blinked yellow and blue as it reviewed his files and then shone bright green before unlocking the door.

"You've been a very good Boy, 1124562. Welcome to cycle number 3,285. Please make your way to the Dressing Hall and prepare for class."

62 was out the door and sprinting down the tunnel before the Keeper finished its sentence. His heart pounded in his chest; he had to find 99 before the doctor from Level 2 did. He rarely noticed how similar all of his brothers looked, but now he panicked with the realization that

spotting 99 in the crowd of hundreds of Boys was going to be nearly impossible.

62 stopped pushing against the other Boys when he reached the entryway to the Hall. Although it was against the rules, he climbed up on one of the bins near the wall and stood up. From here, he was able to look over the heads of dozens of Boys all at once. Throngs of identical heads of brown hair filled the narrow entryway. A sea of bobbing brown eyes looked up at him while they passed.

Then, he caught a glimpse of a bright red right cheek weaving through the crowd. It was the same cheek he saw every morning; the remnant mark of a sleeping boy who always slept on the same spot of his extended arm without moving throughout the night.

"99!" 62's voice cracked as he shouted for his brother. As soon as his voice left his body, he noticed the doctor walking against the tide of Boys in his own search for 99.

99 looked up at 62's perch and changed his course, slowly parting the sea of Boys and coming diagonally across the hall. The change in his route saved him for the moment as it prevented him from walking head-on into the doctor. 62 jumped down and waited for 99 by the wall, relieved when his brother finally broke out of the mob and joined him.

"What's going on? Why do you look so weird?" 99 rubbed a piece of sleep from his eye.

"See that Man over there?" 62 lifted his chin and stood up on his tiptoes to look in the direction of the doctor who was now talking to another Boy.

"Yeah, is he some kind of teacher?" 99 raised up on his tiptoes too, and as soon as 62 noticed his head bounce above the crowd he pulled him down again.

"No. He's called a doctor. He's a bad Man." 62 looked around frantically trying to find a way to escape.

"Men aren't bad. Only Boys are. Everyone knows that." 99 pulled his arm from 62's grasp and got up on his toes again. "What's he doing?"

"He's looking for you." 62 took hold of his brother's tunic and pulled him along the far wall, ducking down so he couldn't be seen behind the Boys getting into line for the showers.

"For me? How do you know?" 99 followed less cautiously, only ducking down low enough to keep 62 from choking him from the tight grasp on the front of his tunic.

"He was at my cube this morning and I heard the Keeper tell him you had an anomaly." 62 stopped near the front of the line and cut in between two other Boys. The Boys moaned sleepily but didn't force him or 99 back out.

62 turned back to his brother as they both reached for fresh tunics. "Do you dream?"

99's eyes opened wide, and his mouth dropped. "Who told you?"

62 shook his head. "It doesn't matter. If you dream, that doctor is going to come and try to make you stop. It isn't good. We've got to get to class and tell 71 before that Man finds you."

The two Boys noticed the doctor turning in circles near the door, confused by the mass of faces surrounding him. He yelled something to a Keeper, and the Machine raised its hand, pointing directly at 62 and 99. The doctor from Level 2 looked from one Boy to the other, then locked his eyes on 62 and smiled the same deviant smile he had when 62 had been strapped to the table in his lab.

"We have to get out of here, right now." 62 bolted ahead of the line, pushed through the opening to the showers and raced past them into the classroom tunnels. He turned, panting, and grabbed at the air behind him but no one was within arm's reach. 99 was nowhere near him. 62 looked up to the showers where 99 had stayed, obediently waiting in line with the others.

The doctor reached 99, placed his hand on his shoulder, and grinned. 62 watched as the Man spoke to his brother, directed two Keepers to take hold of his arms, and began escorting him away.

The Hiccup 36

62 waited by 71's desk instead of sitting in his seat like a good Boy. He wasn't concerned with following the rules right now, and didn't care what the other Boys thought of him standing at the front of the class when the tones rang. 71 strolled in just before the last tone sounded and the door clicked shut behind him.

"Take your seat please, 1124562." 71 fumbled with his tablet and sat down in his hover chair. When 71 looked up again to find 62 still leaning over his desk he responded with a firm tone. "62, I asked you to sit down."

"You have to come with me. 99 is gone. The doctor took him!" 62 reached across the desk and grabbed at the teacher's tunic. He was ready to pull the teacher from his chair and rush him to 99's aid.

"Let go of me, Brother."

71 looked at 62 with such a grave expression that the Boy lost his grasp on his teacher's tunic. 62 took a step back from the desk with tears in his eyes.

"Why won't you help?" 62 felt a tear trickle down his cheek and he wiped it with the back of his hand. "99 needs us."

"We can't hold up the rest of the class for this trivial matter." 71 stood up from his desk and pointed to 62's desk, gesturing for him to sit down once more. "Class, today we are going to discuss the basic structure of the Community. Before I begin my lecture, are there any questions?"

62 trudged toward his desk and sat down with a dramatic thud. Burying his head in his arms, he cried while the other Boys either stared in curiosity or looked away in discomfort. He was consumed by the thought of 99 being taken on a white stretcher through the unmarked tunnels, up into the elevator and into the lab on Level 2. Imagining his brother succumbing to treatments while he and 71 sat in class upset him so much that his crying turned to hiccups.

"The Community is like a program that you would find written on the memory of any Machine..." 71's back was to the class and he was pointing at a diagram projected on the wall.

"*Hic*!" The sound escaped 62.

"... and as a Machine cannot function without a program..."

"*Hiccup*!" 62's shoulders jumped.

"... we likewise cannot function as a group without the Community."

"*Hic*!"

71 turned and shot 62 a warning look. "The Community gives us the parameters of what is good and bad..."

"*Hiccup*!" 62 stopped wiping his tears and slapped his hands across his mouth.

"... and helps us to understand our place in the grand design of Adaline."

"*Hic*!"

"Boy 1124562, are you quite done?" 71's face flushed red and he slammed his hand against the top of his desk. His tablet skipped with the vibration, and the image on the wall flickered.

"I don't - *hic* - know how to -*hic*- make it stop." 62 held his breath until his cheeks burned and his eyes felt like they would burst out of his skull.

"If you will not compose yourself, I will be forced to call a Keeper. Do you understand?" 71 folded his arms and stood like a tower amongst the Boys.

"No, I do not understand!" Rage boiled inside of 62. "I don't - *hic* - understand why we aren't doing something about 99. - *Hiccup*! - I don't understand why you aren't helping him - *hic* - the way you helped me - *hic*. Why won't you talk to me about him?"

"Enough of this. In the tunnel, now. Boys, I will return momentarily." 71 marched to 62's desk, grabbed him by the collar and dragged him out into the tunnel.

"Why are you - *hic* - doing this?" 62 was sobbing now and each time he hiccupped a dribble of mucus bubbled and oozed from his nose.

71 turned away from 62 and looked down the tunnel toward the pods. Then suddenly he spun around, jumped at 62 and yelled, "BOO!" 62 jumped backwards and his heart skipped a beat. The startle interrupted his crying, and he stood staring back at his teacher in shock.

"That should cure those confounded hiccups. Now, about the rest of it. We are here in class learning about the Community instead of running to rescue your brother because that is all there is to do." 71 paced angrily, each step pounding the floor like a piston.

"But I saw him leave with the doctor. You know how to get to his room on Level 2. We can go save him the way you saved me." 62 was too worried about his brother to notice that his hiccups had, indeed, vanished.

"Yes, if 99 had been taken without the proper reporting procedure, as you were, that is something that we could do. But unfortunately for us, that isn't the case." 71 spun again to look at 62 but this time instead of leaping and shouting, he simply looked bewildered. "99 came to me several cycles ago to tell me that he could dream. I was amazed! Two boys in one animation batch with the creativity to dream? It does not happen, unless one Boy teaches the other and 99 insisted that he had no instruction."

"I wanted to tell him about my dreams, but you said not to trust anyone with my secret." 62's teary eyes looked up at his teacher.

"I told him what a rare gift it was that he had, and that I could help him cultivate his ability if he was willing. But he was not." 71 hung his head.

"So he told a Keeper he had an anomaly?"

"No. I did. He wanted the dreams to stop immediately and asked me to repair him. I filed my report and approval for treatment. He has just been waiting these last few cycles to be retrieved."

62 and his teacher stood together, both weary and saddened by what they knew would come next. 71 kneeled down and held 62 in a brief embrace.

"I must return to class. Please join me and let's fill our minds with more useful things."

71 opened the door and entered the room, leaving 62 alone in the tunnel to grieve.

The Resolution

37

62, 71, and doctor 42 sat facing one another at a small table in a shared dream. The Poa Pratensis grew green and thick between the toes of their bare feet, and the sky shone bright and blue above them. Despite the obvious growth in 62's creative mind, all three figures sat in grave silence with worry written on their faces.

"I still don't understand why he wouldn't try to dream more." 62 shook his head and wiggled his toes. Although his heart was heavy with thoughts of his brother, he couldn't help but enjoy the sensation of the prickly spines against his skin. "I mean, dreams are scary sometimes. But they are also wonderful."

"Some of us just don't desire to deviate from the system." Doctor 42 leaned back in his hover chair and sighed. "I know it took me a long time to come around."

"The Community, and all of its systems, are safe. There are no unknowns. Everything happens exactly as it should, in the time that it should. It's terrifying for someone with limited independence to think of deviating from the existence given to them by the Community." 71 looked at the doctor and lifted an eyebrow. "What was it that convinced you to open your mind to the possibility of deviation?"

"Two things, really. First, I discovered that the Community was trying to control even our most basic functions. I was a part of an experiment where we were tasked with trying to implant chips into the lungs and hearts of infant Boys to see if we could get their breath and heartbeats to beat in unison."

62 and 71 both took a deep breath, a half second apart and then looked at 42 with a questioning gaze. 42 shrugged.

"It would have been a success, had it not completely disrupted the adrenal glands and put stress on the heart valves. Of the thousand Boys we tested, only three survived. It left me jaded to submission."

The group paused for a few moments, thinking about the fate of nine hundred and ninety-seven of their brothers lost to the idea of conformity.

71 finally broke the silence with a clearing of his throat. "And what was the second thing?"

42's grim visage lifted into a smirk. He winked at 71. "You've spent our entire lifetime going on and on about how I should open my mind to the possibilities of a little creative thinking. I had to start using my imagination to come up with a way to get you to shut up."

The two Men laughed and slapped one another on the shoulders. Seeing the brothers enjoying their conversation lifted 62's spirits...until he realized that he wouldn't share another moment like that with 99.

"I just wish that I could have talked to him about it. Maybe I could have shared my dreams with him so he'd know how great they could be." 62 slumped in his hover chair.

71 leaned across the table and rested his hand on 62's arm. "There isn't anything you could have done. He made

his decision before he had any data. It's an impulsive flaw in Men."

"And it's even worse in Boys," the doctor added. "Boys haven't lived long enough to learn the value of research and logical conclusions."

"I'm logical." 62 protested.

71 smiled gently. "You're curious, not logical. It isn't the same thing, but it is certainly a good start. Without asking questions and trying new things, you can never know what the possibilities are."

"Okay, well I do have a question." 62 looked from one Man to the other. "Will 99 come back? I mean, if the treatment works and he doesn't get hurt too bad?"

42 leaned forward, suddenly appearing less relaxed. "It is possible that he would be released back into C.A.T. once his injuries are repaired. But I must tell you, I have never seen a Boy fully recover. The electroconvulsive procedure used to treat the dream anomaly does unbelievable damage to the brain and body. And any Boy who does not regain full function following the treatment will not be allowed to return."

62 and his elders fell into contemplative silence again. 62 decided that one day, he would go back to Level 2 and make the doctor pay for what he was doing to 99.

He could feel the heat of anger swell in his heart.

The Containment

38

Each morning 62 rushed to search for 99 after his disappearance with the doctor for treatment. He would race to the Dressing Hall and scan for his brother. When 99 wasn't waiting in line for the showers, 62 hunted for him in the tunnels. When he couldn't be found walking through the tunnels, 62 hurried to the classroom to see if 99 was there. For nineteen cycles, 99's desk sat abandoned. On the twentieth day, it was no longer there.

The tones sounded and no sooner had 71 turned to address the class with a greeting than 62 shot his hand up in the air. "Welcome, class. I would ask if there are any questions, but it appears that there are. 1124562, what is your question?"

"What happened to 99's desk?"

All of the other Boys in the room looked around, suddenly realizing the absence of their brother's desk. It bothered 62 that he was the only one who ever noticed changes like these, but he pushed away his annoyance and focused on the teacher.

"Unfortunately, 1124999 will no longer be attending classes with us." 71 locked eyes with 62 knowingly.

62 frowned but nodded that he understood. He looked down at his tablet and turned it on, then off, then on again. His foot tapped the floor nervously as he fought to hold back tears.

71 started forward as if to offer his sympathy. Before he crossed the distance of the classroom one of the Boys on the other side of the room raised his hand.

71 stopped abruptly and addressed the Boy. "24, your question?"

1126224 rushed through his question with excitement. "Was 99 bad? I didn't think he was bad, but he went away and isn't coming back. What did he do?"

71 sighed. "99 was a good Boy. He simply wasn't feeling well and left to get the issue remedied. Unfortunately, he is not able to return."

"He was unwell?" 25, who had been seated beside 99 for quite some time, looked terrified. He gaped at his brothers and added, "I heard that sometimes a Boy can get unwell and then all the Boys around him get unwell too!"

There was a brief gasp in the room followed by a dozen voices echoing, "Yes, was he unwell? Will I be unwell, too?"

62 glared at the Boys around him, all concerned only about themselves. He was disgusted at their lack of concern about their missing companion. He hunched down in his seat and focused on the blank tablet screen in front of him, drawing lines and shapes upon the white background and doing his best to ignore the petty exchanges around him.

The teacher made his way through the escalating chaos of the class until he stood close enough to his desk to tap the screen of his tablet. The wall behind him illuminated and a large grid appeared. 71 cleared his throat to regain the focus of his students, and when that failed, he shouted, "Excuse me!"

The roar of voices quieted to a low murmur. 71 cast a warning glance at the few remaining chatterboxes in the room and finally the class fell silent. 71 turned to the wall.

"An excellent question has been posed: the question of communicable diseases." 71 drew lines across the grid until there were several rows of boxes outlined. "Let us assume that these boxes represent your cubes. These sections between each box all house an intricate filtration system that removes 99.9987% of common allergens, viral agents, bacteria, and other disease hosts."

On another section of the grid, 71 drew what was clearly a floor plan of the large Dressing Hall. "The tunics that you pick up here in the entrance of the Dressing Hall are all embedded with nanotechnology. These microscopic nanobots tirelessly patrol your bodies day and night to remove microbes, bacteria, or bodily secretions that could, in the right circumstances, cause you to become unwell.

"The showers themselves also spray a combination of hydrogen and oxygen that has been infused with antimicrobial, antifungal, and antibacterial compounds which further prevents illness."

71 turned to face the classroom and raised his hands in the air. "The only possible way for me to pass an illness on to you, or for you to pass an illness on to me, is for both of us to exchange bodily secretions directly from our eyes, noses or mouths. This is why C.A.T., and indeed all of Adaline, frown upon physical contact from one Man or Boy to another. As long as we do not invade one another's personal space, it is statistically impossible for disease to exist."

A hand rose in the corner and at 71's nod a small voice creaked, "But then how do Boys get unwell?"

"An excellent question. While we do all that we can to prevent illness, it is true that occasionally Boys and Men do become unwell. This can be due to any number of causes, but most frequently it is found to be due to an internal anomaly within an individual." 71 paused as each Boy looked around the room and then down at his own chest to try to spot any anomaly among them.

"The majority of anomalies are benign, meaning that they never become an illness and never exhibit any symptoms. An anomaly may be as simple as having a few too many or too few hairs upon one's head or may be as complex as having conjoined organs. Major anomalies are typically identified and resolved prior to animation. Minor anomalies that progress to illness later in our lives are addressed as they become a concern."

"What do we do if we find an anomaly?" 12 shouted the question out as he felt around his ribs through his skin.

71 looked back at 62 and answered seriously. "If at any time you feel you are suffering from an anomaly, or you are feeling unwell, you are required to notify either your teacher or a Keeper of your condition."

62 looked up from his tablet at last, a trickle of tears visible on his cheek.

The Visitor 39

The silence of the pod was broken by the tiny beep of buttons being pressed outside 62's door. 62 opened one eye and lifted his head slightly to see who or what was accessing his data panel. He couldn't get a view of anything but the blue glowing words and numbers scrolling across the sign above his neighbor's cube across the hall.

```
Cycles since animation... 3,650... Height...
139.4   centimeters...   Weight...   32.564
kilograms ... C.A.T. Result: Unknown.
```

The beeping noises outside 62's cube ceased, and the door slid open. A Man 62 didn't recognize reached in and attached a small sensor to the back of his neck where 62 knew his data chip was implanted. Through the slit of his partially open eyes, 62 could see a long black cable strung between the sensor and a scanner box that the Man held in his other hand.

"No, sir. All vitals are within normal range. It doesn't appear that his data feed has been tampered with." The stranger whispered into a small communication device he wore on his head.

62 could hear the faint buzz of another voice leaking out of the earpiece. The stranger nodded. "Yes, sir. I will continue manual monitoring during rest. No, there was no response when I applied the electrode. The Boy still sleeps."

The stranger pulled the communicator headphones from his ears and gently removed the sensor from 62's neck. As he wound the cord up and put the scanner box away in a pouch on his back he whispered, "I certainly hope that you are not being tampered with, little Brother. If you are, this could be a very long road for both of us."

62 lay still and silent while he waited for the stranger to creep back out of the cube. A few beeps sounded and the door slid closed before the soft padding of bare feet on the hard floor signaled the Man's exit. Once he was a few paces away, 62 crept up to the door and looked out the small opening. The stranger's shadow disappeared into the darkness before 62 could see where he was heading.

As 62 craned his neck and leaned closer to the door, his hand slipped and touched a sensor on the wall beside him. Not realizing his error, he jumped at the startling voice of the Keeper who responded to the signal.

"Boy 1124562, are you unwell?" The Keeper's eyes glowed yellow as it stared in at 62 and extended its hand out to extract his data from the port beside the door.

"No, thank you. I am well." 62 looked away from the Keeper and craned his neck again to look down the hall. "Who was that Man?"

"All Men are secure in their pods to rest. Are you unwell?" The Keeper's eyes flashed green and yellow as it began to download.

"I am well. Thank you. I just woke up." 62 sat back down in the center of his cube.

"Do you require assistance returning to sleep?" The Keeper leaned against the screen on the door and the click of its fog dispenser rang in 62's ears.

"No, I don't require your assistance. I will rest now." 62 laid down and closed his eyes. The Keeper ended its connection with his data stream and moved away into the darkness.

62 remained still and silent, but he could not quiet his mind enough to fall asleep. He didn't know how a Man could have entered his cube without the Keeper knowing of his presence. With hundreds of thousands of sensors in the pods, it should have been impossible for a Man to pass through the halls unnoticed.

A flicker of lights and the sounds of breakfast overcame 62 before sleep returned to him again. In nervous exhaustion, he put away his blanket and waited for his meal to drop through the chute. Like he had done hundreds of times before, he followed his brothers through the halls and tunnels in seamless repetition of the morning ritual.

Standing in line behind hundreds of brothers in the Dressing Hall, each exchanging their dirtied tunics for clean ones, all standing like a wall of mirrors against one another, 62 felt lost.

His desire to dream, learn and create dissolved in a great wave of despair.

Unlike the orderly Boys around him who each stood up straight, sleepily pointing their chins up and out in indistinguishable obedience, 62 slumped his shoulders and hung his head. The visit from the Man in his cube extinguished his drive to be different and, at the same time, brought to light all the ways his existence was different from those around him.

None of the other Boys 62 knew had ever received private tutoring from a teacher. Neither had any, except 99, mentioned the ability to dream. Not once had he caught a glimpse of another Boy scribbling drawings on the margins of his tablet, nor had he witnessed them openly argue with either Man or Keeper. He was fairly certain that none had escaped the deadly treatments on Level 2 and was confident that no one else received secret visits from Men in the quiet time of rest.

62 looked up at the Shower Aide looming above him and let the cleaning fluid run into his open eyes. He expected the liquid to sting—had hoped that it would burn his eyes and distract him from the empty emotions brewing inside of him. To his surprise, the liquid did not burn and instead spread a cooling sensation over his gaping eyes. The flow of the clear liquid did blur his vision, and he stood in awe as for a moment all of the stiff fixtures around him were given the illusion of bending and flowing in an imaginary breeze.

The shower ended and he shook his head, forcing the illusion from his eyes. As he made his way to his classroom, he wished to be like all the other Boys. If only he could be unconcerned with the goings on of Adaline. If only he could stop the dreams. If only he could stop worrying about his brothers. If only…

His thoughts were interrupted by the ringing tones of class, and the clearing throat of his teacher at the front of the room. 62 turned on his tablet in unison with the rest of the students. But when he looked up at 71, he didn't see the same plain old Man that his classmates saw. 62 noticed the teacher's unusually puffy eyes. He observed a tired lisp creep into the Man's speech. And when 71 extended his hand to point at the day's schematic, 62 was the only Boy who seemed to notice the long, dark, angry slash extending from the teacher's wrist to his elbow.

The Surveillance

40

It took some time for 62 to enter his dream, but he did finally make it into his subconscious. Once the falling sensation ended and he found his footing, he imagined the small pinhole of light that 71 normally opened to connect to him. A faint speck glowed in the air in front of him and he focused on his teacher, trying for the first time to make the connection himself.

"Hello?" 62 pressed his mouth against the light and hoped that 71 was on the other side. He did his best to focus on the defining features of the Man, his long flowing beard, his sparkling brown eyes, and the long narrow gash on his forearm. "Are you there?"

"I am." The whisper came through so softly that it was hard for 62 to know if he had imagined it, or if it were actually there.

"I hope that this is you," said 62. "And I hope that you are all right."

"I hope that I am me, as well," the small voice replied. "If I'm not who I am, or if you are not who you are, then I fear we are both in trouble. But, to ease us both do you know Chobham?"

"I do. Will you join me?" 62 moved away from the light and surrounded himself in the darkness of his dream.

"It's impossible." 71's voice was quiet, but the sound of defeat was unmistakable. "They are watching me closely now. If I jump, they will know."

"What happened to your arm?" 62 asked the question with hesitation.

"I was attempting to reach through but found myself in the wrong dream. Once I discovered my error I pulled back, but the person on the other side grabbed hold and wouldn't let go. I had to force the connection to close before I had made it all the way back."

62 held his hand over his mouth, astonished. The light faded but then shone brighter as he focused, trying to imagine the Man's tired face. "I thought that we couldn't be hurt here."

"I thought the same," came the reply. "But it's clear that I still have much to learn about the connection between our mind and body. The wound is most certainly real."

"Can I try to come to you?" 62 wasn't sure how to make the transfer from his dream to 71's, but he desperately wanted to see his teacher.

"You could, but it would be dangerous for both of us. The monitors in my cube are all active now. Even if I twitched with the effort, I'm afraid they would know." 71's speech faded as if he had turned his head away from the light to look behind him.

62 was suddenly distracted by the feeling of something on the back of his neck. He moved his hand to brush the sensation away and became aware of the hand pressing a small electrode to his chip. He fought the urge to wake up and instead stood still and rigid in the dark. The distraction averted his focus enough that the pin of light that connected him to 71 faded to darkness.

All that 62 could hear was the sound of his own measured breathing. The disembodied hand that pressed the sensor to his neck grabbed hold of his arm and moved it gently to his side.

"Hush, Brother." The strange voice rung in his ears. "This will only take a moment."

62 held his breath and started to wake. His lungs began to burn, and his mind was dizzy with the sensation of moving from dream to reality. His eyes fluttered open to the dim blue light of the open door, and the unmistakable feeling of a large Man's body pressed against him in the tight confines of his cube.

"Who are you?" 62's voice was groggy with sleep.

His question startled the Man, and he could feel the tug of the cable connected to his neck as the stranger pulled away slightly. The cube was silent aside from the sound of close breath.

"I am a maintenance Man." The reply was uneasy, as if it were being answered for the first time.

62 turned his head slightly and could see the outline of the Man's face in the blue light. The maintenance Man was much younger than 71. His beard was dark and thin against his jaw line, his eyes flashed with secrecy and his thick hair looked black in the dim light.

"Why are you here?" 62 rubbed his eyes and tried to seem as drowsy and weary as possible despite the urge rushing through his bones to get up and run away.

The Man cocked his head, considering the question. "I'm just doing my job. I got a call that there might be a malfunction, and I came to check on it."

62 tugged at the sensor on his neck. "A malfunction here, in my cube? It seems fine to me."

The maintenance Man nodded, light bouncing off of his cheeks as they moved up and down. "Like I said, just doing my job. Now, go back to sleep."

62 mirrored the stranger's reassuring nod and closed his eyes. He didn't return to sleep though until well after the Man had put away his scanner and snuck back out of his

cube. When he did finally reenter his dream, he again focused on 71 until the opening between them shone in the darkness of his mind.

"Is it you?" 71's voice rang with panic.

"It is me, and I know Chobham." 62 pressed his face into the small ray of light and tried to show himself to his teacher. He didn't know if his features would shine through, but the warm light on his face had a calming effect. "There was a Man here, a maintenance Man. I noticed him last cycle, too. He says he had a report of a malfunction in my cube."

"What was he doing?" 71's face pressed into the other side of the connection. Lines of worry were visible, even in the brightness of the warm light.

"Both times, he put a sensor on my neck and read my data with a scanner." 62's hand brushed the still sticky spot where the cable had been connected.

71's head shook from left to right. "This is not good, Brother. The Community must suspect you've been tampered with. We must not connect our dreams any further. There is no telling what they will do if they discover us."

"What do I do if he comes back?" 62 was filled with dread as the teacher began to pull away.

"Just be a good Boy. Speak of it to no one, not even me when we wake. This is just not good." 71's face shone with worry as it faded away.

The light between the Boy and his teacher went out, and 62 found himself alone in the dark once more.

The Inspection

41

The cycles were excruciating without the break of time spent in dreams. 71 looked more haggard as time went on. It was easy to see that the lack of sleep overwhelmed him. His lectures became less passionate, more tedious, and many of the Boys yawned with boredom during class.

62 did his best to stay in line and follow the rules. The Maintenance Man continued to come, waking him in the quiet of night. No matter how many times 62 asked the Keepers who the Man was, they continued to report that no Men were in the pods.

Rarely did 62 speak to his teacher anymore. The void that the absence of their friendship left was felt by both of them. From time to time, 71 would ask a question in class and look at 62 with begging eyes, and 62 answered with long winded replies that wandered off of the topic at hand. Otherwise, 62 understood that he needed to treat his teacher like a cold acquaintance.

62's existence was lonelier now than it had ever been. The repetition of each day grated on every nerve and drained every emotion. He felt as devoid of personality and expression as the other Boys in his pod. He tried to convince himself that this was how it was intended to be.

Cycles passed, his knowledge of the Community grew, and 62 began to only think of what career he might be placed in. He did still love the classroom and began to think again on hopes of a career in Education. Although his experiences made him more familiar with the internal workings of the human body than most Boys, he was sure that he did not want to become a doctor.

He was pondering the differences between doctors and teachers in the Dressing Hall when a group of Men appeared at the head of the line to the showers. 62 peered around the restless bodies ahead of him to see 71 and the doctor from Level 2 in deep discussion.

62 slunk down behind the Boy ahead of him in line but then thought he must be too far away for the Men to notice him. Emboldened by the distance between them he moved out of line just far enough to gain a better view of the two Men. He stretched his left foot far out beside him and pointed his toe at his place in line. Although the Boy behind him rolled his eyes, his space remained open and waiting for his return.

As each Boy passed by, the doctor would take him by the collar, lift the hair on the back of his neck and inspect it briefly. Once the doctor released each Boy, 71 would smooth his collar and straighten his ruffled hair before gently returning him to the line. A pair of Men stood at the entrance to each set of showers, making sure that no Boy went unchecked.

At the head of 62's line, between concurrent inspections and reassurances, the bad doctor and 71 argued with one another. At first 62 couldn't make out their words, but soon the line moved forward until 62 was close enough to hear them. He ducked back in line so he wouldn't be noticed.

X-CURSE

"You really expect me to believe that a Boy with such wild and erratic vitals could suddenly become so average?" The Doctor from Level 2 hunched over a terrified Boy and grunted as he stared at another bare neck.

71 retrieved the ruffled Boy from the doctor's grasp. "There, there. All is well, Brother. Now, run along like a good Boy and head off to the showers." The teacher looked up at his companion. "I don't expect you to believe anything. All I know is that you are upsetting my students with your incessant hunt for anomalies that don't exist."

"Oh, they exist all right." The doctor's tight grip on his newest victim caused the Boy to cry out in pain. "I won't stop until I can prove it. And so help me, if you are involved in some type of data tampering, I'll do everything I can to send you off to some labor sector where you'll never be heard from again."

71 responded to the threat by smiling with kindness at the teary-eyed Boy standing between them. He patted the Boy on the back. "You have passed your first test of the day, young brother. Congratulations! Dry those eyes and head off to the showers." The Boy nodded and scurried off as 71 waved the next Boy forward.

"You know, Doctor, it is strange that you accuse me of tampering with the data of this Boy when he was taken into *your* lab for treatment. I would think that you'd be more enthusiastic about your ability to finally have cured someone of an anomaly after so many failed attempts." 71 chuckled.

The doctor's neck and cheeks flared red with what 62 knew was anger. "I will have you know that I am a very successful doctor who has treated hundreds of patients! How dare you!"

The angry outburst was well timed. 62 was next in line and the doctor was so distracted by his frustration with the teacher that when he grabbed 62, he forgot to look at the scars on his neck. 71 pulled 62 gently out of the doctor's grasp and played at smoothing his tunic and hair.

"I'm sure you are successful, Doctor. That's precisely why I'm astounded that you are so upset over a Boy you have obviously cured." 71 turned his back on 62 and worked at prying the next victim from the doctor's grasp.

"Don't you patronize me with your praise, you old dusteater!"

The doctor's temper boiled over and he lunged at the teacher. His fists landed first on the old Man's jaw, and then his stomach before several Keepers responded to the disturbance. Boys began screaming, crying, and running in all directions to get away from the scene. 62 used the distraction as an opportunity to move closer to the showers ahead of several preoccupied Boys.

The area echoed with the roar of the doctor's rage, the excited shouts of hundreds of Boys, and the mechanical assurances of dozens of Keepers. Above it all, 62 could distinctly make out the gleeful laughter of his teacher.

The Disruption

42

62 ran his hand along the place where he knew 42 had replaced his data chip. The skin was smooth and soft now, as if there had never been a cut there at all. He smiled to himself as he got in line for the showers, knowing that the skin had healed so well that the scar was nearly invisible. So far, none of the Men doing inspections had found it.

It was a good thing that the unauthorized procedure had healed completely. The Boys were now being checked for signs of tampering every cycle. The physicals varied in intensity, and 62 never knew from one day to the next if he would be poked and prodded by Men in Defense uniforms or simply receive a second scan by a Keeper to make sure his data stream was consistent with previous reports.

Regardless of the intensity of the searches, two things were certain in 62's mind. First, it was clear that no one was going to make it to class on time. Each cycle since the inspections began, 62 had barely walked through the classroom doors when the tones rang to dismiss them. All of the testing and lectures were at a standstill. Teachers simply had no students to teach, and even when the Boys made it to class, they were too nervous about the changes around them to pay attention.

The second certainty was that one Man's obsession was overwhelming the Community. The Doctor from Level 2 obviously had a lot of power to be able to shut down the efficiency of C.A.T. for so long. Each cycle that passed the Boys, and even the Men, became more unruly. The tenseness that filled the hallways of C.A.T. was unlike anything 62 had experienced before.

The lines crept along, millimeters at a time. Although the Dressing Hall had always teemed with Boys before class, now it was constantly overcrowded. Hundreds of bodies pressed against one another. While 62 was able to close his eyes and imagine that he was in a vast place all alone, his brothers did not have the same luxury. They had no imagination.

62 refused to open his eyes when he heard the shuffling feet, raised voices and crack of knuckles on soft flesh. C.A.T. had never had an issue with violence before the inspections, but now fights were a regular occurrence. When the first scuffles had taken place, the teachers voiced their fear of being outnumbered by the students and insisted that the Community do something about it. Now hundreds of Men from Defense patrolled the pods, halls, and tunnels. Any Boys found fighting were taken away to find the anomaly making them violent. When the medical staff couldn't locate any deviation in the offenders, they simply told the Keepers that each Boy was bad.

Then came the fog.

The problem was that no deviation was ever found among the Boys throwing punches. Each of them was found to be perfectly normal as soon as they were removed from C.A.T. for observation. They each accepted their punishment obediently. The fog was both administered to and suffered by the offenders without dispute. When the fog sleep faded, the Boys were returned to their pods. Within a few cycles, their complacency wore thin, and they began to fight again.

It was like a virus spreading unchecked through the pods. The more the Community tried to contain it, the worse the violence got. No one seemed to know what was going on. No one, that is, except 62.

For the first time in his young life, 62 was glad he knew how to leave the stress of C.A.T. to explore the recesses of his imagination. As soon as the Boys started to be regularly checked for anomalies, he could see the flash of anger settle into his brothers' eyes. He could see the heat in their flushed skin and hear the hiss of resentment in their voices.

As 62 imagined his open spaces, he felt one of his brothers bump him. Several other Boys, who had also been pushed aside, began to grumble. Shouting and pushing rose like a wave in the sea of Boys around him.

"Close your eyes and just think about something else." 62 said to the group around him without opening his eyes. "You'll feel better."

The reaction from the Boy closet to him was the same as so many others since the militant checks began. "Close my eyes? You must be blowing dust. He bumped into me, and I was here first!"

"Just try it. It could save you both from the fog." 62 opened his eyes and took in the group fighting around him. "Quiet, all of you. You're going to get in trouble!"

Fists flew above his head and 62 caught the grazing blow of a knee as one Boy kicked another. 62 shut his eyes tight and took a deep breath. Staying as still as possible, he hoped to avoid injury from the throng of bodies around him. He waited in silence for the area around him to clear. One by one, the aggressive Boys were plucked from the fight and taken away.

The space around him felt large for a moment as a dozen Boys were ushered away. But as soon as the group dissolved, more Boys shuffled in to join the line, waiting to have their necks checked.

The Conversation

43

62 sat in his pod listening to his brothers sleep. There were fewer snores than before, and the breathing of those that were left sounded strained and halting. All of C.A.T. was on edge from the constant suspicion of tampering. So many Boys had been transferred to Level 2, being tested for anomalies that didn't exist, 62 had had enough.

He had been trying to connect with 71 for several cycles, both in dreams and out of them. Not much conversation could be made under the scrutiny of the Defense Men though. The only time 62 saw his teacher was in brief spurts when he made it through the lines in time to attend class.

71 appeared more tired than the Boys had ever seen him before. 62 knew that much of the weariness in him was from missing so many hours of sleep. But there was more than that. The new procedures the teacher had to follow for instructing his class were exhausting the old Man.

Each portion of the lessons now had to be described in detail to a Man from Defense in real time before it could be given to the class. That meant that 71 had to have his lessons planned and memorized verbatim. Every section they covered, 71 had to leave the classroom to go into the hallway with his assigned Defense Auditor. The Auditor was required to listen to the lecture and approve or deny the segment. Once approved, 71 was allowed to return to repeat it, word for word, to the class.

The tampering investigations also continued and 62 couldn't stand it anymore. Everyone was on edge, confused, and frustrated with all the new rules and restrictions. Looking around at the fidgeting bodies and glassy-eyed stares of his distracted brothers, 62 realized he was the only one among them that understood why everything had changed. The Doctor on Level 2 was *really awful*—and he was the only one who knew that.

Someone had to stand up and put an end to all this stifling control. Wasn't there anyone in the Community who would do that? But then, if 62 was the only one who knew who was behind the problem…maybe it was up to *him* to do something about it.

But he was just one Boy. What could he change?

He had to try.

When the rest time came, he sat in the dim light of his pod in silence, waiting for the Maintenance Man to return for another scan of his chip. Eventually, the quiet was punctured by the sound of a Man's feet stepping gingerly through the pod.

62 had pretended to be asleep every other time the Man had come. This time, he stayed sitting awake and alert in the center of his cube. The Man's shadow passed by the window as he reached the panel to open the door. There was a pause, and then the Man leaned close to look into the dark cube.

"Oh, hello," the Man uttered in surprise, not expecting his target to be awake. He shuffled around outside for a minute, pretending to be busy with the panel by the door.

"Hello, Maintenance Man. Welcome back." 62 sensed the Man was going to leave. "Please, come in. I know it's a tight fit, but I don't mind. I want to talk to you."

The Man stopped fidgeting and leaned against the window grating. "You do?"

"Yes. I want to find out if I can help you get back to your pod." As 62 spoke, the Man looked surprised. 62 added, "All of you. I want you to go back to working in Defense, so that I can go back to learning in C.A.T."

"I'm not supposed to talk to you. I'm only supposed to download your data." The Man shrank back into the shadows as if to leave.

"What if I let you download my data while we talk?" 62 offered. "Then you won't get in trouble for not doing your job."

62 heard the chime of beeps outside his cube and the door slid open.

"Okay."

The Maintenance Man leaned into the cube and stretched his arm behind 62's neck. He carefully attached the electrode in his hand to the place where he knew the data transmitter would be. He gently unwound the cord attached to the device and plugged the other end into the scanner.

"So, what do you want to talk about?" The Man asked.

"Who makes you come download my data every night?"

The Man looked 62 steadily in the eye. "Why do you want to know that?"

"I want to let him know that I'm tired of him interrupting my rest." 62 tried to sound confident even though he was trembling inside.

The Man let out a laugh. "I've been telling him that this is a waste of time for the last ten cycles, at least."

"Then why does he still make you do it?" 62 leaned forward to make it easier for the Man as he adjusted the electrode to get a better connection.

"He has his orders, and we must follow them. It's just the way it is." The Man shifted, trying to get more comfortable in the tight space.

"But, why? I'm just a regular, average Boy." 62 could feel his heart jump as he demanded answers, but he didn't worry. He knew that the modified chip wouldn't transmit any elevated vitals on the scanner.

"Let me ask you a question. Has anyone ever told you about the other levels?" The Man whispered.

62 thought back to his experiences on Level 2 and B15. He wouldn't tell this stranger that he had not only heard of other levels, but that he'd actually been there.

"Yeah," 62 replied. "Before all of this, our class was learning about the history of Adaline. I saw a picture of it."

"Well, let me tell you how this all works." The Man breathed in 62's ear to make sure no one could hear him. "The higher up in levels someone is, the more important they are. You're just a Boy all the way down here in B32. I've got instructions from a Man on B11, and he has instructions from Level 2. So if you want all of this to stop, you have a lot of levels of people to convince."

"Level 2?" 62 asked.

"Yes. Level 2. Nobody up there cares what a Boy thinks. About anything."

62 nodded. He knew the Man on Level 2 and knew that he had to find a way to make him stop.

The Plan 44

62 spent several cycles coming up with a plan. When the idea came to him, he wondered why he hadn't thought of it sooner.

Before he could do anything though, he had to talk to 71. When he was ready to put his plan into action, he hung back after class. Luckily, 71 was forced to wait until the classroom was empty before leaving, another new security measure to make sure that Boys were under constant supervision.

62 approached 71's desk. The teacher averted his gaze, pretending to be busy looking at some dust collecting in a seam in the wall behind his desk. "71, I need your help."

71 glanced at 62 briefly, then used the sleeve of his tunic to wipe the offending dust away. "Troubles with your testing?"

"No, sir. I need to know how to get into other people's space."

71's eyes darted toward the door where he knew the Defense Auditor was waiting. "It's against the rules to enter another Boy's pod, you know that."

"Maybe it is, but maybe it isn't a Boy I'm trying to get to." 62 spoke in a low voice, just above a whisper. He picked up his tablet and pointed to the screen, so it looked like he was asking questions about class, in case anyone was paying attention. "And maybe I wouldn't try it when we're awake.

"You can't do it." 71 shook his head. "It's too dangerous. They'll catch you."

"I've got to do something. Everything that is happening is because of me. Because of *us*." 62 leaned in closer to his teacher. "I know the risks. But I think I know a way to stop all of this."

"Stop what?" 71 eyed 62 suspiciously. "I don't think you know exactly what is happening here. You can't get into the dreams of all the Men in charge of Defense. Even if you could, you wouldn't find anything there. I doubt if any of those brutes have an ounce of imagination. There's no dreams to get into, Brother."

"I don't need to enter all of their dreams. Only one of them. And I know he dreams because he's been in mine." 62 was so close to his teacher that he could feel the Man's nervous breath on his cheek.

71 nodded. "I suppose you're right. I will tell you. But you must promise that you'll be careful. We don't know what he will do if he sees you."

62's face was serious. "I think I do, and it's okay. He's the one who needs to be careful."

The Power 45

62 waited until he couldn't possibly hold his eyes open any longer before he allowed himself to rest. He wanted to make sure that he would fall into sleep quickly and completely. What he was going to try to do was more difficult than anything else he'd attempted, and he didn't want to waste any concentration on trying to get to sleep.

Listening to the sounds of heavy breathing seeping through the walls of his cube, 62 closed his eyes and allowed himself to fall into the darkness. It took a moment for him to center his mind and stop the quick falling sensation of unfocused dreaming. Once he was able to right himself, he imagined a dense steel floor to stand on. As soon as his feet hit the ground, he set to work.

"This is a really stupid idea," 62 spoke to himself, "but might as well give it a try."

He sat down on the floor. Leaning forward, he placed his elbows on his knees and rested his face in his hands. He closed his eyes tight, focusing on creating a pinhole of light to connect with another dreamer. He thought long and hard about the Man he wanted to see. He imagined his short grey beard, hard brown eyes, and long white coat. He remembered the menacing expression on his face and the eerie precision of his practiced hands.

He thought about the Man in his room, full of devices, surrounded by bustling Keepers. 62 was frightened as he remembered being tied down to a bed, the Man hovering above him. He shook, feeling the tingle of imaginary electrodes on his head while needles jumped on phantom dials beside him.

He felt his consciousness shift as the landscape around him melded into the scene in his mind. 62 opened his eyes to find the torturous room forming before him. He gasped as three Keepers appeared, each displaying images of Boys broken by electrical current.

The Keepers surrounded a bed. They leaned over it and pushed the arms and legs of a thrashing Boy down to the mattress. One by one the flailing limbs were tied down to the bed. The gentle hum of electronics filled 62's ears. One of the Keepers picked up two wands connected to wires leading to a large box with dials and gauges.

62 cried out at the dream. "No! No, stop it!" He flew up from his place on the floor and rushed the Keepers. Overwhelmed by panic, he pushed the Machines aside to get to the bed. He tried to tear away the metal bands that held the Boy down but couldn't get them loose.

He came to the strap that held the dream-Boy's head. It was unmoving and connected to several electrodes. 62 pulled at the metal with all his might, grunting with the effort. He wanted to free the Boy. The Boy who looked up at him knowingly. The Boy with tousled hair and soft, tired eyes. The Boy who was smiling. The Boy who was...

62 gasped. "You're me!"

The dream Boy smiled. Although his mouth didn't move, his voice echoed in 62's head, "You know what to do."

62 let go of the bands around the other Boy's head, closed his eyes again and focused. The dream melted, dissolving into complete darkness except for a tiny speck of light pulsing ahead of him.

He pushed his hand against the bright light and willed the pinpoint to open. Slowly, the light grew in both size and intensity until it enveloped his hand. 62 pushed harder.

The shift from his own dream to the Man's consciousness was instant and disorienting. 62 stumbled as he fell onto a large black and white grid. Hulking figures rose into the air around him, still and imposing.

"Rook to H-4." A voice rang from somewhere in the distance.

The black column beside 62 began to move, slowly dragging from one square to the next. The grating sound of metal on metal filled the air. 62 covered his ears with the palm of his hands to escape the painful screeching.

The doctor walked along the edge of the board, following the column with his eyes. He came to rest behind a line of white statues. The screeching noise stopped as the column entered its assigned square and the room fell silent. The doctor looked at the grid sternly, not seeming to notice 62 standing where the tower had been.

"Pawn to G-3." As the doctor spoke, one of the white statues slid forward two squares on the grid, screeching against the floor.

The doctor from Level 2 walked back to the edge of the board where most of the black figures stood. As he passed by this time, he noticed 62.

"Who are you?" The doctor halted his stride mid-step as he demanded an answer.

"I am the Boy you are looking for." 62 spoke slow and clear.

"You what?!" The doctor shifted back on his heels, startled.

"I am the Boy you are looking for. I've come to tell you to stop looking."

The doctor laughed, an unsettling crack that escaped like static. "You are nothing but a blip in my imagination. Be gone." He gave a dismissive wave.

62 stood, as motionless as the statues around him.

The doctor clenched his fist and shouted. "I said, be gone!"

"Having some trouble?" 62 asked with calm confidence. "Maybe I can help you, if you'll agree to stop bothering with C.A.T."

The doctor tilted, off balance. "Stop bothering with C.A.T.? Those Boys need a good bothering. That teacher..." he shook his head in frustration. "My *brother* is tampering with their data. I just have to find out how."

"I'm the one you are looking for." 62 repeated.

"You are no such thing. You are just my imagination run amok. I will find out what's happening. I'll discover the truth!" The doctor thrust his fist forward, shattering the short pillar in front of him.

"I know the truth." 62 said. "Would you like to hear it?"

Instantly, the doctor's rage vanished. He looked at 62 with pleading eyes. "Tell me. Please tell me the answer."

"You are the one damaging C.A.T. You must stop tampering with the Boys and let them return to their studies."

The Man's rage returned, displacing the uncertainty that filled him a moment before. "I am the solution!" he shouted. Turning to view the rest of the grid he spoke again. "Knight to D-6."

A figure with a long curving neck started to shift across the board. 62 closed his eyes and willed his imagination to overpower it. The giant figure stopped, turned around and began to creep toward the doctor. Its slick black enamel faded to the color of pale skin. Hair grew from its head, and it opened its eyes.

A perfect copy of 99 said, "You are the anomaly."

The doctor stood, astonished. He whispered, "What?"

Another pillar transformed into another Boy from 62's class. 62 and both of his copies reached their hands out toward the doctor. Their mouths opened and they spoke in unison. "You are the anomaly."

62 focused on three more figures lined in a row directly in front of the doctor. All three transformed, their pale fingers reaching out to touch the doctor's tunic. "You are the anomaly."

"This can't be happening." The doctor put his head down and watched his feet as he walked toward the opposite corner of the board.

Five more figures transformed from towers and columns into copies of Boys 62 knew. As the statues transformed, they followed the doctor. They groped the air behind him, some of them reaching out to grab at his back and arms.

"Don't say that! It has been a burden all my life, but no one knows. They can't know. I've told no one." The doctor spat at the new group of duplicates. "I'm going to find a way to end this affliction once and for all."

"You didn't have to tell anyone. You show them whenever you appear in their dreams." 62 forced one of the Boys to say.

"I've seen you," each Boy said, one voice rolling over another in a wave.

"No, that's not true. No one believes what they see in their dreams. They don't know it was me. No one can know." The doctor pressed against the wall of his dream. A door opened revealing his sterile office on the other side. He slid through the door and tried to shut it behind him.

As the remaining statues opened their eyes, becoming 62, they crowded the door. The mass of arms and legs pressed against the door, breaking it off its hinges. "We know," the Boys spoke together.

"You cannot know!?" The doctor shouted at them. "I am a doctor! A repairer of Men. I must find out what is changing Adaline and stop it."

The doctor fell backwards as the throng of Boys pressed into the room, hitting the edge of his exam table. 62 opened his mouth to speak and each copy did the same. Their voices rang out together in a powerful melody. "You are the anomaly. You are destroying the Community. Stop now."

The mob of Boys parted so 62 could pass through them. He entered the small, white room and stood beside the doctor. He could see sweat beading on the Man's brow and could sense his heart racing. 62 and each copied Boy cocked their heads in curiosity as the doctor scrambled to get to the far end of the table.

The doctor trembled, and a single tear trickled down his cheek. "I must find the problem."

62 reached his hand toward the doctor. "I know the truth. Let me show you."

The doctor's hands trembled beneath the sleeves of his lab coat. His eyes shone with unshed tears and his lip trembled. He looked so small, so lost within himself, and then a shadow of relief passed over his features. He nodded in compliance and reached across the table to grasp 62's hand. "Okay. Show me."

62 held the doctor's hand tight as two of his copies slammed the Man's wrist into one of the locking cuffs.

The air whooshed out of the doctor's lungs as he gasped in surprise. "What is this? Untie me, right now!"

The multitude of copies followed 62's motions as he leaned forward to whisper, "You are the problem with Adaline. Stop, now."

"Let go of me." The doctor squirmed, his arm caught in the tight cuff around his forearm. He gasped, "I can't make it break free."

62 smirked. "Of course you can't. I won't let you."

The doctor's eyes went wide. "You aren't a dream. You're real."

"Yes, I am." 62 focused on the hand he held tight. "Doctor, all this time I've been afraid of you. Of what you could do to me. But now, I'm curious. What are you most afraid of?"

He concentrated, willing himself to draw energy from the doctor in order to increase his ability to control the Man's dream. The surge of power that leapt from the Man's hand and into 62 almost knocked the Boy off of his feet. He regained his balance without letting go. "I'm sure you know what every Boy is afraid of. I think Men are afraid sometimes, too. Even Men like you."

A sinister smile overtook the doctor's face, and he stopped struggling for a moment, allowing 62 to get an even firmer hold without him noticing.

"Of course I know what you fear." The doctor's sneer widened as the Boys in the room began to grow. Their skin became tight and shiny. Their eyes glowed and the room filled with the smell of synthetic skin and hydraulics.

"Boy 1124562, are you unwell?" The now-Keepers chanted together. A dozen sleep-fog ports clicked open, and tendrils of sticky fog began pouring out of them, filling the small room.

62 didn't falter. He focused on the doctor's hand and drew more energy from it. "Yes. The Keepers are scary to me. To all of us. But these Keepers aren't real, are they? I asked you a question, Doctor. Are you going to answer it?"

The doctor's face fell as the Keepers around him succumbed to 62's control. Each mechanical head tilted towards the Man. "Doctor, are you unwell?"

62 allowed the Man just enough control to see what would flicker across his imagination. He held his hand tight as the Keepers lifted the doctor up on the bed and forced his free arm and legs into the heavy straps.

The Keeper closest to the doctor looked at 62 and chirped, "This Man has an anomaly. It cannot be repaired."

The doctor's hand became sweaty against 62's palm, and his slick fingers began to slip free. 62 grabbed the doctor's wrist with his other hand. "Don't go, Doctor. You haven't shown me what you are afraid of yet."

The Man's eyes flashed with burning anger. "You can't do this. This is *my* dream. You're just a Boy!"

62 looked at the Keeper that was diagnosing the doctor. "What happens next?"

The Keeper spoke, the same level tone eerily unfeeling. "Anomalies must be removed from Adaline."

The room around them winked out of existence. Suddenly they were being pushed along a hallway. Transportation Aides were on all sides, pushing the doctor's gurney so fast that 62 struggled to keep up. Still, he held the Man's hand tight.

The doctor began to panic, and all of the lines around them became crisper as he lost what little control he had left of the dream. The lights shown in blinding brightness, their stinging white rays glimmering off the bodies of the Transportation Aides as they rushed past.

"No," the doctor gasped. He pulled hard at the buckles on his hands and feet, kicking and twisting with increasing panic. "Don't make me go there."

"Go where?" 62 panted.

There was a blast of air around them as the scene changed again. The gurney stopped and the Machines vanished. The Man, still strapped to the bed, writhed in terror as a large metal door appeared.

The door had no window or handle. It was surrounded by wide, steel panels and hundreds of thick rivets.

"What's so scary about a door?" 62 let one of his hands loose from the doctor and reached out to touch it. The metal burned with a hissing sizzle under 62's skin.

The doctor yelped. There was a crash in the air high above them. 62 gazed up and saw a tangle of arms and wires racing down on them. A single eye radiated red from the center of the ambling mess.

A high-pitched voice rang out all around them. "Hello. Thank you for participating in Adaline. You have an anomaly. Please, be a good Boy and enter the containment unit."

Two of the long, segmented arms reached out from the middle of the mass of wires and hoses. Their claw-like hands clamped onto the edge of the bed. The large metal door opened with a whine that rang in 62's ears. He had to fight the urge to let go of the doctor's hand so that he could cover them.

A flame licked the air just inside the doorway. Its light flickered across the faces of a hundred Boys. They looked out at 62 with terror in their eyes. 62 backed up a step, and the Boys noticed the doctor. Upon seeing him the throng of Boys leapt up, trying to get out of the door through the climbing flames.

"Doctor!" they cried out. "Help us!" Flames wrapped around their arms like shackles and kissed their pale faces until they blistered. The whole room glowed red, and the cries of the Boys grew louder as the roar of flames tried to hush them. A tone of sadness rang through the air and melded into a melody of pain like 62 had never heard before.

The doctor thrashed against the gurney as the Machine above them pushed him toward the gaping mouth of the flame-licked door.

"No!" Tears welled in the Man's eyes and his skin lost all of its color. "I'm not unwell!"

The hot fire singed the end of the exam table. The synthetic sheet popped and sizzled in a mass of tiny black bubbles as it curled and melted into itself. Black smoke wafted up from the smoldering wheels as they inched farther into the gaping doorway.

The doctor's eyes rolled inside his head, finally coming to rest on 62. As if just seeing the Boy for the first time, he gasped. Through trembling lips he whimpered, "Don't let them take me, 62."

62 closed his eyes and wiped the overhead clamps, glowing red eye and echoing mechanical voice from the dream. He allowed the fire to die, and the anguished faces to fade into the darkness. He left the door as it stood, yawning open on newly slacked hinges.

X-CURSE

All was quiet aside from the doctor rasping and wheezing in the bed. 62 still held his hand, and the doctor squeezed it in thanks. A deadness filled 62's heart as he looked at the pitiful doctor beside him.

"So, this is your fear." 62 laid his free hand on the now cool door. "This place in your dreams is what haunts you."

The doctor leaned up as much as his confines would allow. "Why did you do this, Boy? Why did you make me come here?"

62 inspected a rivet so he wouldn't have to look at the doctor in disgust. "I didn't bring us here, Doctor. You did. But now that I've seen it, I can imagine it."

62 felt the doctor squirm under his grasp. He continued to speak without looking at the Man. "I can bring you here whenever I want. I can make the Machine push you in there, and let the fire eat you up."

The doctor laughed, nervousness cracking in his voice. "Fine, bring it back here."

62 finally looked back at the face of the Man whose hand he still held. "I could let all of those Boys out. I can make them do to you whatever treatments you did to them."

As 62 thought of the Boys he had just seen, their silhouettes surrounded the doctor's bed. Each Boy held a different medical device in his hands. The doctor eyed each scalpel, wire and tube with wariness.

A moment of silence passed before the doctor breathlessly spat, "It's just a dream. It can't hurt me. Not for real."

62 squeezed the doctor's hand in both of his. His fingers dug into the Man's flesh as he allowed the anger to burn inside of him. "Oh, but I can make it real."

62 began to break the link between their two dreams. The doctor's eyes went wide as the darkness approached them, creeping inch by inch from the edge of 62's consciousness.

"Let go of me." The doctor squirmed, his arm still caught in the cuff of the exam table. His eyes were bright with fear.

"You think you have all of this power, but you don't." 62 pulled the Man's hand another inch towards his side of the closing rift. The darkness closed in so that it blocked the doctor's face from view. 62 refused to let loose the wriggling fingers that tried to escape his hold.

"Please, stop." The doctor pleaded as the darkness closed on him, just above his wrist. 62's closing dream cut the Man's flesh like a knife.

62 waited until a trickle of blood ran down his wrist before letting go. The doctor wrenched his hand backward into his own dream, cutting his hand further. 62 could hear him cry out in pain on the far side of the small white light that was left in the hand's absence.

"Doctor, be careful letting your Keepers look at that. Now you have a physical anomaly. You never know what they might decide to do to treat you." 62's voice echoed in the darkness of his own mind. The light shrank smaller until it was the size of a speck of dust, and then it winked out of existence.

62 stared at the spot where the light had been. He was so overcome with emotion that he hardly noticed the touch of a Man's hand on the back of his neck, or the quick sting of an electrode as it connected to his data chip.

The Recovery 46

The changes in C.A.T. weren't immediate. A change in protocol rarely is. It didn't take long, though, for the Boys to notice fewer Men patrolling the halls. The constant checks for anomalies changed to every other cycle, then every tenth cycle, and finally, none at all.

62 wasn't sure if C.A.T. would ever go completely back to normal, but he was glad for the extra freedom that he and the rest of his brothers now shared. There was still the occasional Defense Auditor found strolling between classrooms, and the Keepers all seemed to retain their hypersensitivity to any changes in the Boys' behavior. But all in all, life was a lot more relaxed than it had been.

It took dozens of cycles before 62 could convince 71 that it was safe for them to share dreams again. Once they started visiting in sleep, though, it quickly became a part of each cycle.

"I don't think we have to worry about him for a while." 62 sprawled out across the broad fluffy Stratocumulus Cumulogenitus that he had imagined into his dream.

"Who, the Doctor from Level 2, or the Maintenance Man?" 71 turned his hand over in the soft denseness of the puffy air beneath him and watched the tiny grey particles swirl between his fingers.

"Either of them, really. I talked to the Maintenance Man before I went into the doctor's dream. He said his orders came from up on Level 2." 62 tried not to feel the emotion that his teacher called 'cocky', but he couldn't help it.

The doctor had awoken from his dream with a slice in his skin from his elbow to the tips of his fingers and had been so panicked about it that he blabbed the whole dream to anyone who would listen. He'd come to 71, begging the teacher for help in curing his dreaming anomaly. He called 71 an 'expert' on the subject. A nearby Transportation Aide overheard the conversation and relayed the report to the Community. 71 had simply watched as the doctor was whisked away by his own Keepers, carried off to be treated by the hands of some new doctor on Level 2. 62 wouldn't have believed it when 71 told him about it later on, except that afterwards the Maintenance Man stopped coming to download his data.

"So you're saying that they're in cahoots?" 71 interrupted 62's thoughts with his question. The teacher rolled over and pressed his face into the cool mist of his student's dream.

"Where is cahoots?" 62 practiced closing his mind off from his teacher's and suddenly surrounded his consciousness with a thick steel box. Everything within the box remained as it was, albeit substantially less expansive. Everything outside of the box became pitch black in the void left outside his imagination.

"It isn't 'where is cahoots'. The proper question is, '*What* is cahoots?'" 71's voice echoed in the emptiness that sprawled between them. As suddenly as the steel beams and thick walls had appeared, they vanished again, and 71 found himself seated on the puffy Stratocumulus Cumulogenitus aloft in a bright blue sky beside his student once more.

"You are getting very good at that," the teacher noted.

"Thank you. So, what is cahoots?" 62 rubbed his hands together and a small black book appeared with a thin yellow writing utensil.

71 blinked in astonishment. "What is that you have there?"

"A book. I created it to take notes in. I keep it in a secret place in my mind so that I can look through it and remember things." 62 turned to a blank page and scribbled the word "Cahoots" along the edge of the page.

"Ingenious!" 71 clapped his hands together in delight. Then, remembering the question, regained his scholarly visage. "Cahoots means that two or more Men are in league with one another. That they are working together toward a shared goal or purpose."

62 scrawled the definition across the page, filling it with unskilled handwriting. It had taken some practice, but the words were getting easier to write, and easier to read. 62 hoped that some cycle he would be able to produce text as legible as what he had seen in other books. With the definition of cahoots recorded in his ledger, he laid the writing utensil down, closed the book around it, and pressed his hands together until the journal disappeared with a small puff of smoke.

"So then, are we in cahoots?"

"I should say that we are," 71 mused. "But then, what are we cahooting for?"

62 thought for a long time before answering.

"I guess we're in cahoots to try to make being different okay. Like you said at the beginning of class, we all look the same on the outside, but we have differences on the inside. Some Boys are smarter or faster or funnier than others. Some of us work hard and others don't work at all. We all are different in the way we act. And I think that some of us want different things than others." 62 thought back on all the things that 99 had said about wanting everyone to be the same. The sadness of it made him shake his head.

"I don't think I could have said it better myself." 71 nodded.

62 looked up at the bright blue air above him and imagined that he could see the faces of his many brothers smiling and laughing in the swirling sky. He liked to dream about them and promised himself that he would do it more often.

"But how do we teach Men like the doctor from Level 2, or Boys like 99 that it is good to be different?" The laughing faces above 62 vanished and were replaced with the visage of the Boys trapped behind the fiery door from the doctor's twisted dream. 62 sometimes thought he saw 99's face pressed against the flickering flames.

"It is simple, little Brother. All we can do is keep trying." 71 reached across the short distance between them and picked up 62's hand in his own.

"Do you think it's real?" 62 stared at the doctor's steel doorway. Painful cries filled the corners of his consciousness as the specters of lost Boys grasped at the air.

The teacher squeezed the Boy's hand tenderly for a moment and used a surge of shared energy to push the grim scene from the dream. 71 shook his head. "No. Although I doubt our friend, the doctor, had much of an imagination, I also doubt that anything like that could be real. I suspect it is just his consciousness teaching him a lesson."

62 sat up. "But what if it is real? What if there are Boys that need help?"

71's cheeks spread into a soft and reassuring smile. "Don't get lost in the terror of a mad Man's dream, Brother. Use your imagination to expand your mind and do good in Adaline. Without imagination we are nothing but a collection of cogs helping to turn the wheels in a giant Machine. It is our dreams, our loves, and desires, that make us Men."

62 looked down at his hand, firmly clasped in his teacher's. The sensation of warmth and transfer of energy

between their fingers was shocking in a way that was comforting and wonderful. It was so different from the feeling of holding the doctor's clammy hand. He squeezed his teacher's fingers in response to the empowering gesture.

"I will always dream," 62 stated simply, "And I will never give up."

62 comes back in BOOK 2 of

The X-CLONE Secrets:

X-CAPE

Keep reading to try out the first chapter of the second book.

X-CURSE

ABOUT THE AUTHOR

Dire Kepler was born beneath the dark shadow of Mount St. Helens after its eruption. Her ashen arrival in the Pacific Northwest exploded into a life of tall tales and high-stakes adventures. A natural storyteller, Dire began writing novels in her early twenties and never stopped. She has published dozens of novels, novellas, and short stories. Her words are devoured worldwide by readers hungry for a little justice.

Best known for dark psychological thrillers as author D.K. Greene, Dire started writing science fiction early in her career. After years of exploring the sinister side of humanity, she has come back to her dystopian roots with *The X-Clone Secrets*. With a love of oppressive robotic regimes and casts of defiant characters, Dire is right at home surviving in the chaos of any collapsing dystopia.

When she isn't writing novels, Dire spends most of her time with family, traveling the western coast of the United States, and consuming other people's stories.

You can follow Dire on her website at https://varida.com/direkepler or send her an e-mail at dkepler@varida.com.

X-CURSE

X-CAPE

CHAPTER 1

Even before he opened his eyes, he knew this was the end.

By the close of the next cycle, Boy 1124562 would be ejected from The Career Aptitude Testing center. He threw off his blanket and sat up, feeling the buzz of energy grow around him. As each clone woke up in his individual cube, and remembered they were leaving, the excitement in the air thickened until 1124562 felt the particles of anxiety and wonder press into him from all directions.

Finally, 1124562, simply called "62" by his closest brothers, had developed enough to do more than just listen to lectures and stare at diagrams. He and hundreds of other Boys animated in his batch would be moving to the Training and Skills Kinesiology center.

62 turned his thoughts inward and shook his head in silence. He almost hadn't made it this far. Nearly 250 cycles ago, he had embraced the powerful secret of his anomaly, his ability to dream, and found the strength to battle the doctor who had wanted to eliminate it. The dreams in his head might make him an aberration, and he'd be in immense danger if the wrong people found out about them again, but

they gave his life meaning and 62 didn't know how his brothers survived without them.

He stretched his arms overhead. It wasn't much of a stretch; elbows bent, and knees locked within the narrow walls of his cube. But it felt good to move. He smiled up at the ceiling as he thought back with satisfaction on what he had just dreamed. He had been in a vast space, surrounded by books, and had spent hours devouring the stories within them. How all that knowledge, and all that *room* fit inside his head, he didn't know.

He reached out to the small opening in the wall to collect his breakfast tablet and downed it with two gulps of the thick drink from the tube that hung beside it. 62 was excited about the promise of new surroundings, even if he'd be leaving his closest brother behind. His teacher, Man 2871, was 62's best friend, the one who had helped him understand the gift of dreams. Without his help, 62 might have disappeared in a foggy cloud of discipline and reprogramming a long time ago.

A shiver ran down 62's spine. Whether it was from the anticipation of his upcoming transfer, or the fear of the sleep fog that the Keepers used to subdue bad Boys, he couldn't tell.

His thoughts were interrupted by a pair of flashing eyes peering through the grating of his cube door. "You've been a very good Boy, 1124562. Welcome to cycle 3,896. Please make your way to the Dressing Hall and prepare for class."

As the Keeper pulled away from the door, it unhooked from his data port and its eyes dimmed slightly. It was easy to tell when the Keepers were watching a Boy closely. Their eyes flashed in sharp bursts of color as they processed incoming information and calculated a response. The data passing through their processors burst with sparks of intelligence that made them seem alive and powerful. But as soon as they were no longer connected to a data port or streaming information through contact with a Boy's skin, they became nothing more than a collection of mindless Machines.

62 exited the cube and traveled shoulder to shoulder with the other Boys of his pod toward the giant Dressing Hall. Just like they had every day since they came to C.A.T., they would shower, change clothes and head to the classrooms. When 62 and his brothers first arrived in C.A.T., there had been a lot more room to move around. The area had never been spacious, but after so many cycles together, the Boys' growth was apparent. All of the empty spaces had been filled with identically bony elbows, lengthened feet, and widening shoulders.

The throng of Boys passed by the Keepers, Shower Aides, Transportation Aides, and other Machines without acknowledging them. They were just Machines; tools humming in the background to keep the clones' lives in order. But when 62 stood in his shower, he wondered what his new home would be like. What Machines would be there? And just how would he be looked after, especially in his sleep? 71 wouldn't be there to protect him if his dreams were discovered. The thought sent a shiver through him just as the cool liquid of the shower, infused with microscopic nanobots, cleaned his skin and repaired any nicks or scratches. He shook his chilled body and pushed the spark of fear from his mind the moment the faucet stopped spraying. The cold only lasted until the Shower Aide blew warm air over him to dry whatever liquid remained. His shower complete, he moved forward in the line to put on fresh clothes.

62 didn't pay much attention to anything around him until he entered his assigned classroom. Aside from his dreams, where he had discovered almost anything was possible, the classroom was where he felt the most alive. He made his way to the back of the room, the hover chair bobbing slightly beneath him as he dropped into his seat. Tones rang through speakers hidden behind smooth white walls and just as the door was about to slide shut, Man 2871 appeared.

71 had a few more wrinkles around his eyes, and slightly less hair around his gleaming head, than he'd had on 62's first day of class. The teacher maintained the same flourish as that first day though. His arms waved and his beard wagged as he greeted his students.

"Good cycle, brothers. Welcome to the beginning of the end." 71 winked, a facial expression that 62 and most of the other Boys still struggled to master.

"Good cycle," all nineteen Boys echoed back.

"This cycle, we will begin reviewing your basic knowledge of Adaline in preparation for your transfer. Before we begin, does anyone have any questions?" Two wild eyebrows crept up 71's forehead. His crisp brown eyes darted around the room before settling on the tablet in front of him, waiting for the flashing buttons to appear as questions were formed.

It only took a second before 71's tablet was aglow with a dozen blinking lights. He tapped his finger on the device. "56, your question please?"

"What is the Training and Skills Kinesiology center? I thought after C.A.T. we'd be assigned straight into our careers." 56 sat up straight, his hands folded neatly in his lap. There was not a single crease in his tunic, and his brown hair laid perfectly across his forehead. He'd been telling his brothers that he was sure he'd be assigned a career in Defense.

"In C.A.T. our innate knowledge is tested. We learn about the Community in terms of theory and hypothetical conditions. Your tests have been tracked throughout your time here, and by now the Community has a good idea of which career you'll be placed in." 71 swiped his hand along the screen of his tablet, throwing an image onto the wall behind him.

The picture was of two Boys standing across from one another in a large circle. Both Boys faces were partially obscured by their raised fists. They stood with legs wide, knees bent, their rear heel lifted as though ready to charge their opponent. Although the two Boys appeared identical, the one on the left seemed to be enjoying himself more than the one on the right. 62 had seen those expressions before. Back when the doctor from Level 2 had discovered 62's ability to dream, he forced all of the Boys to be checked for anomalies. The stress of constant surveillance took its toll on everyone. As tensions grew, fights had broken out. There wasn't always a decisive winner or loser, but sometimes one Boy was so comfortable with fighting that his opponent looked at him with the terror of inevitable defeat.

A bubble of guilt grew in 62's gut when he thought about the doctor from Level 2. It had been risky, but with help from 71 he had learned how to get into the doctor's dreams. By showing the deranged Man his own nightmares, 62 had convinced him to leave C.A.T. alone. The plan had worked, but in the end, the doctor was taken away for a treatment that 62 knew would be difficult for anyone to survive.

He wondered who he'd meet in the new place. Would the clones there be kind, like 71? Or cruel like that doctor? And what if, somehow, the new tests made his anomaly visible? 71 had taught him to block his thoughts from outsiders but what if there was someone, or some*thing* in the new place that found out his brain was faulty and got into his dreams?

"... and so because you haven't put any of these theories into practice, you will now be tested practically. The Head Machine must know what physical attributes you possess before it will make a final assignment for you. Intelligence will help you in any of the careers, absolutely. But if you have both intelligence and innate physical strength? Well then, you're going to grow up to be the kind of Man we need to lead us into the future."

"So, we're basically just going to find out if we're good for Defense or not?" An overconfident smile crept along the corners of 56's mouth.

"Oh no, much more than that. The Men who toil to maintain Adaline also need incredible strength."

A voice carried through the class from another student too impatient to wait for his turn. "You mean, you have to be strong to dust things?" A rolling wave of giggles erupted.

"Now, now." 71 patted the air in front of him to hush the room. "Every career in Adaline is important. If we all worked in Defense, we'd probably have to stand all the time because there would be no one to repair the hover chairs when they malfunctioned. If we were all brilliant enough to be employed in Education as I am, then... well, I suppose that would be perfection. Who wouldn't want to be me?"

Laughter erupted throughout the room, this time without smirks hidden behind hands. 62 laughed, too. Most of his brothers believed they knew where they would be placed based on the testing and awards they had received in C.A.T. 62 was the only Boy in his classroom that had even scores across all their subjects. He had even won such a variety of awards that there were no clear career types for him to fall into. Although he didn't know what the future held, 62 hoped to become a teacher just like 71.

"94, what was your question?" 71 boomed over the laughter, and the noise quieted to a whisper.

"What is Kinesiology?"

"A fantastic question!" 71 swiped through several screens on his tablet before finding a diagram and pushing it up onto the wall. The image was of a nearly naked Man with cables and data receivers connected all over his body. The Man appeared to be running in place while a doctor typed data into a Machine nearby.

"Kinesiology is a study in how our bodies move. It considers our skeletal, muscular and neurological structures and deciphers which type of movement best suits our bodies. It's a fascinating area of study." 71 stared at the photo with awe equal to that of his students.

"But aren't we all the same?" 94 looked around at the Boys seated on either side of him.

"As always, that answer is both absolutely, and not quite." 71 flicked his wrist and the image of the two Boys about to fight with each other reappeared. "Although we are virtually the same, there are small differences in the way we move. One Boy might be slightly faster than another. One Man may have more clumsiness than his neighbor. Although their strengths may be strikingly similar, no two bodies are ever exactly the same."

The class of cloned Boys looked skeptically at their teacher. As if on cue to suspend their eager curiosity, the tones for the end of class rang out. Several of the Boys burst out of their seats and rushed the door. The rest remained behind, slowly shutting off their tablets and putting them away neatly.

"A shining example!" 71 shouted above the din. "Notice how each one of you moves at your own pace. Some are fast, some are slow, even though you all eventually get to where you're going. Observe how you move! Ah, 75, see how you bumped into the desk there? Oh, and dropped your tablet? Fantastic!"

62 shook his head, amused by the teacher's commentary. He joined his brothers as they poured out into the hallway, lost in thought as the crowd pushed him back toward his cube.

To read more, pick up BOOK 2 of

The X-CLONE Secrets:

X-CAPE